Weakness

by Dana Pratola

Also by Dana Pratola

DESCENDED
Jett
Sebastian
Aaro
Ulrick

Standalone
K-I-S-S-I-N-G
Like a Country Song
The Haunting of Josiah Kash
Weakness
The Covering
I Kissed Kevin's Girlfriend
Heart of the King

ACKNOWLEDGEMENTS

GOD: I know some may think it's silly to thank You on my book page, but I will take every opportunity there is to thank You. Without You I would have nothing, and I am so grateful.

FAMILY: Yeah, you guys all know how I feel. Love squared.

FRIENDS/READERS: I am humbled you even give me and my work the time of day. And Cecilia (Marie)... WOW. You're the absolute best. Thanks so much for your help and support.

CHAPTER 1

WHEN SHE BENT OVER, I almost swallowed my tongue. She put a pitcher in the washer, then straightened, turned.

Serena. Not my type, with her delicate frame and features, blond and blue ponytail, and that perpetual smile she aims in equal portion to every customer. But I'm accustomed to seeing her now, cheery and eager, and like a gulp of clear morning air, I find her refreshing. I can't help looking at her.

Her blue eyes flicked to me, then darted away, and her smile faltered for a second before she fixed it in place and shifted her gaze back to mine. Had she always done that and I never noticed?

"Good morning. Can I help you?" she asked.

"I already ordered."

"Oh, all right."

This was the first time she'd spoken to me since I started coming here three months ago, though I often hear her talking to customers and co-workers. I like her voice, musical and lilting. It reminds me of stories I read when I was in the service, of music in the air in Ireland. I don't know why. Lack of sleep playing with my head, making me punchy, I guess.

THE PHONE RANG, AND she twirled in a happy circle before answering. "Good morning, All You Can Brew, Serena speaking, how can I help you?"

She paused, her smile brightening.

"Hey! No, don't worry about it. I'm bringing the blankets, and my sleeping bag if I can find it. I can't wait till Friday. The second I'm off shift ... yeah! A whole weekend away from here. It's been too long since we all got together."

I pretended not to pay attention as a kid behind the counter handed me my coffee. Still, I couldn't help hearing the enthusiasm building in her voice.

"Yeah, I'm going to have the best time, bears or no bears," she said. "I need this. ...Yeah...okay, I'll talk to you later."

When she hung up, she balled her fists and gave a little bounce on her toes, unable to conceal her excitement. My chest gave an answering squeeze. Should've known then.

Moving down the counter to the sugar dispenser, I popped off my cup top. I don't use sugar, but I jabbed a plastic stirrer into the dark brew and twirled it around, stalling my departure as another worker came in from outside. I'd passed her on the way in, talking on her cell. She walked up to Serena with a smile and touched a hand to her back.

"Hey, I hate to ask on short notice," the girl started. "But can you cover for me Saturday?"

Serena's face went blank.

"I wouldn't ask, but my sister's coming up from Raleigh, and I never see her or my niece. She'll only be here for the day," the girl continued.

The muscles in Serena's face tightened and slackened, and her mouth drew downward at the corners. "I ... um...."

"It's my niece's birthday. So cute, that kid. But I only get to see her in pictures."

"Uh...."

I held my breath, waiting for Serena to assert herself.

"Sure," Serena said.

"You're the best! I have to call my sister," the girl said and marched back outside.

My jaw clenched tight. Why would Serena agree to that when she had plans? I decided to find out. It might be selfish, but I looked forward to seeing her smiling face after hours of sitting in a car or tagging along with grim-faced clients. Now she had ruined that for me and I felt slighted.

"Why did you do that?" I asked.

Serena's eyes flashed to mine, widening. "Excuse me?"

"Give up something you want to do to cover for her. Why?"

She looked torn between telling me to mind my damn business, and tears. The first, I could take. Maybe I should've let it be.

"We're friends," she said, so quietly at first, I barely heard her. Then she cleared her throat. "We're friends. We help each other out."

"You *think* you're friends," I contradicted. "Friends don't use you and lie to get you to cover when they know you have something to do."

"What do you mean, *lie*?"

She approached the edge of the counter like a fawn to a sapling. Close enough for me to catch a whiff of her recently scrubbed skin through the aroma of coffee and freshly baked scones. She smelled far more delicious. I set my cup in front of her and replaced the plastic lid.

"When I was coming in, she was outside on the phone, talking about a music festival on Saturday and who would bring the beer. But you would have agreed even if she'd told you the truth." I shook my head, unable to hide my disappointment. "You have a weakness, Serena. You accommodate others instead of yourself."

She stared at me, confusion, mistrust, and hurt churning in her eyes. Okay, I probably should have shut up, but I'd told her, and now I was leaving before I became too invested in her business. I lifted my eyebrows and walked out, leaving the decision to let people use her up to her.

I sat in my car another few minutes, watching as the other girl went back inside, and wondering if Serena would confront her. No, I would bet not. Shame.

FOR THE REST OF THE SHIFT, I wrestled with the idea of asking Joy about the concert but left without saying a word. I sucked at confrontation, and aside from that, I was distracted. The customer—some of the staff called him *Frosty* for his degree of warmth—had spoken to me. To me. Called me by name. It was about something personal that he had no right to comment on, but he'd taken the time to address me and give me advice. Well, if you could call "*you have a weakness*" advice.

I was honest enough with myself to admit he'd shaken me. I'd watched him come in almost every weekday for a few months. It was impossible not to, given his height and a build that made him appear larger than the doorway. And those trance-inducing eyes as deep and rich a shade of brown as the shop's finest brew.

But for all his amazing looks, there was something ... scary about him. Whether because of his demeanor, or that my tongue usually balled up in the back of my throat when he came in, he intimidated me, plain and simple. The few times I'd almost taken his order, I'd chickened out and let someone else do it.

We all wondered what he did for a living. Though he almost always dressed in a suit, he didn't seem the type to sit behind a desk all day. Images of mobsters with shoulder holsters, counting bundles of cash in the back room of a butcher shop, flitted through my brain before I rattled them loose with a good shake of my head. My ponytail came around and whipped me in the eye. Served me right for letting my mind run away.

I parked in front of my house and groaned out loud when I saw my mother's car in the driveway, home early from work. After having my camping trip ruined—okay, ruining it myself—I was in no mood to deal with her petulance or complaining. I gave the steering wheel a last squeeze—my last attachment to my lifeline outside the house—and got out of the car.

My mother's squawky tone carried out to me on the front porch, but she wasn't speaking to me. It seemed one sided. Must be on the phone.

"I don't know what you're talking about," she said. "That person has never lived at this address."

I couldn't help rolling my eyes as I opened the door. Another debt collector calling.

"Do your parents know you make a living harassing people? Don't call here again!" My mother slammed the handset back on the hook. "Damn snakes. How do they expect to get their money from someone who's too broke to pay the bill in the first place?"

"Beats me," I muttered, and headed to my room.

"Hey, you left clothes in the washer again," she said, following.

"Oh. Sorry. I meant to throw them in the dryer, but I fell asleep."

"I had to rewash them."

"Sorry. Like I said, I fell asleep. I shouldn't have started them so late."

"I can't afford to be using extra water with the bills the way they are," she persisted.

I sighed. "I said I'm sorry."

She looked like she wanted to say something else, but three *sorrys* usually put an end to the complaining, and she pivoted on her heel and walked away. The second she was out of sight, I closed my bedroom door and fell back on the bed to stare at the cracked ceiling.

This was pathetic. Most of my friends were out on their own or living with roommates, and here I was still getting bitched at about chores. What twenty-four-year-old had *chores*? At this age, I should have responsibilities of my own and make my own decision to carry them out or not.

Though, I knew what would happen if I had a roommate. She'd be the one planning parties and inviting people over and I'd be the one stuck doing all the dishes and cleaning barf off the shower curtain. I lifted my fists and let them fall to the gray and pink comforter.

Why was I like this? So accommodating. Hardly causing a ripple, even if it was something important to me. I hoped it poured Saturday all over Joy and her outdoor festival. I enjoyed the thought. Until I remembered my friends would be outside as well, camping. No sense ruining their day.

Pulling a pillow over my face, I let out a scream. It was some kind of frustrated roar that came up from deep inside. The kind that could be mistaken for a wounded animal if anyone heard. I couldn't even get revenge in my fantasy! As if wishing for rain or anything else really worked. If it could, Joy would realize what a completely selfish bitch she was, and take her hours back.

Or I could drive up to the campground after work on Saturday and salvage some of the weekend. It was better than nothing. I let out another, more human sound, and called Lisa to tell her about the change of plans.

A few minutes later, I hung up more annoyed than I had been. Lisa was understandably disappointed—well, pissed off—but she'd asked a good question: *Did Joy offer to take one of your shifts in exchange?* No. Not any time she'd asked for a favor. But that insight only made me angry at myself, not Joy. Why didn't I ask her? Because I knew she wouldn't do it. Yet I helped her anyway. Why was I like this, so overly compliant?

When the phone rang in the kitchen, and I heard my mother's voice, I thought I knew. Not to blame her entirely, but she tended to be dismissive, and sometimes harsh, and other times—more often lately—she could lash out like a cyclone. It always seemed best not to rock the boat. Staying out of her way was the best route, but when I couldn't avoid her, bending to her will was the easy way out.

Though, that wasn't a stream of thought I wanted to wade into right now. I sat up and grabbed my phone, walked past my mother's upraised eyebrows, out of the house, and to my car. A drive might help clear my head.

Several blocks away, I turned onto Newbury Street, immediately regretting it. Up the hill, as far as I could see, were brake lights. It was rush hour and traffic always thickened this time of day, but it looked to be moving at a crawl. Must be an accident ahead. What in the world was I thinking coming this way at this hour? I threw my hands up and let them drop into my lap.

After five minutes, I came to the top of the hill and could finally see the problem: an event tonight at the exclusive Milliard Ball Room down the road. Police had one lane closed, funneling cars to the other side to share the road. I nudged into the single lane and followed at a turtle's pace behind a driver who seemed determined to stay exactly in the center of the cones guiding his way.

Passing the packed lot, a man waved flashlights, signaling patrons to parking spots, even though it was still daylight. The building itself was a beautiful plantation house with tall shrubs and ornamental willow trees bowing to brush the luxurious lawn with delicate green fingertips. I'd imagined what it was like inside, since I didn't have the money to find out.

Then I saw a familiar face. *Frosty.* Standing at the door in a dark blue suit, looking cool as ever as he scanned the area. He appeared to be looking for something. Or someone. A woman, I'd bet.

My stomach gave a little squeeze, most likely of embarrassment, recalling how he'd zeroed in on Joy using me. More precisely, on my letting her. Did I appear so pathetic that I needed a stranger to intervene? And still, I'd done the wrong thing.

I drove on as the traffic started to flow again, and for some reason, the classic children's ditty popped into my head. *Frosty, the snowman, had a body like a.... Rock* came to mind. He had a body like a rock. How did a man get a body like that, anyway? Hours upon hours at the gym, yeah, of course, but who had that kind of time? Steroids maybe. I'd noticed him one day, out of his suit, wearing jeans and a tight-fitting T-shirt—as if a shirt could be anything other than tight-fitting on that frame—and ... wow. How could someone nicknamed *Frosty* be so hot?

My mind worked and reworked the song, but I'd taken it as far as I could already, and turned on the radio in an attempt to drive it from my brain. "Damn, I Wish I Was Your Lover" didn't help, and I switched the station. Again and again. Tonight it seemed they dedicated every song to stirring the loins and turning thoughts toward fornication.

I chuckled. That's what my Christian grandmother called it. *Fornication.* Sex with anyone outside of marriage. She had heavily influenced me, despite my agnostic mom. I know there's a God, and have even had prayers answered, but I find it hard to believe He cares whether I listen to rock music, as Grandma claimed. I believe since God knows everything, He knows my heart.

Still, I never had a desire to *fornicate.* The world is much more permissive than it was even when I was in middle school, but I always somehow knew inside that I'm meant for only one man, and that he will wait for me and appreciate the gift of purity I give him. It sounds corny even to me, sometimes, and all my friends call me naïve, but I'm willing to take their jokes and laugh with them, knowing that in the end, I'll be vindicated.

Thinking of *Frosty* wasn't helping any, so I turned off the radio and glanced over at the romance novel on the seat beside me. I like to park near the bridge at Hanson Park—weather permitting—recline on the hood of my car, and get lost in a story. It would be dark soon, but even if I didn't read, I could at least take a little time to breathe. Or think about my life and make myself tense all over again.

Working at a coffee shop will not get me out of my mother's house or into nursing school. I need a job that will pay the rent and keep me fed. Beyond that, I only have my cell phone bill. And car insurance. And repairs, gas, doctor visits as needed.... And back to the never-ending circle that is my life.

I CAN'T STAND RICH PEOPLE. Well, that's not entirely true. I have met a few that were nice, individually. For some reason when they get together, they feel compelled to have a pissing contest, comparing their shiny new acquisitions, accomplishments, even lovers. And it's the same whether they're businessmen or rappers. They're generally a boring bunch. Though the rappers do keep me on my toes when it's sometimes difficult to differentiate friend from foe. I'd almost rather duck bullets at a nightclub, or dodge a crazed fan's ten-inch knife outside an apartment in SoHo than stand here listening to businessmen talk. Maybe it's just businessmen I can't stand.

Warren Peters isn't so bad, though, as the filthy rich go. Realtor to others of his class, threats aren't that common in his field. He'd ignored the first two notes, but after someone shot a round into his headboard as he slept, he'd taken it seriously enough to hire me. He hadn't gone to the police for fear of clients thinking they might be in danger when around him, and if anyone inquired, my presence could be explained by the tens of thousands of dollars in jewelry he usually wore.

I'm no detective—I earn a living protecting my clients from threats, not seeking them out—but it would help if I knew where that threat was coming from. Based on the penmanship of the warning note, it was a woman, but Warren claimed not to know who, speculating it was someone he'd had sex with, dissatisfied with the temporary arrangement.

I'm sure there's more to it than that. Warren doesn't seem the type to lead a woman on or make promises, and only true nut jobs get that attached after one tumble in the sheets. I'm betting it's someone he knows better.

As I stood nearby, listening to Warren and his buddies discuss weekend plans, I couldn't help thinking of Serena and her lost camping trip. I assume she's at least five years my junior, and what a sweet kid. Though, if she isn't careful, being a people-pleaser will become so ingrained in her she'll.... Not my business. As I'd told myself all day. If she wants to let people walk all over her, it's her choice and her problem.

But why did it piss me off so much? And why haven't I been able to forget about our brief exchange this morning? I acknowledge that even though she's not my type, I find her very attractive, but that's not it. Probably.

It might have more to do with my wanting to bring a resolution. It's what I do. I resolve things. When I'd seen a family of eight digging through trash heaps in the Sudan, I'd found them food. When I'd discovered a homeless mother and daughter living under a bridge in an Iranian ghetto, I'd gotten them shelter. I've assisted in the construction of countless wells in Ethiopia, and a young mothers' shelter right here in the USA. Maybe I'm subconsciously viewing Serena as a humanitarian mission. She needs a backbone, and I'd like to see she gets one.

Ignoring the niggling feeling that I was making excuses to see her again, I returned my focus to the room. After tonight, Warren was leaving the east coast for Hawaii and would be someone else's problem. I often travelled with clients, but Warren intended to stay in the islands through the winter, and tremendous pay or not, my time in service had given me a deeper fondness and appreciation for being on the mainland. Specifically, for the solitude of my twenty-two-hundred-square-foot home on my ten acres.

A few more hours and I would be there, away from the false laughter and ego jockeying. Alone. Alone was better than being with the wrong person. Much, much better.

When the night wrapped up and Warren was safely in the hands of the next shift, I finally went home. The fact that my dog, Teddy, wasn't there to greet me, still felt like a wound in my chest, but after a month, it was getting better.

I'd told Heidi a dog was a bad idea, that I'd never had one because I was never home. She would take care of it, she'd insisted. She had. And when she'd left, she'd taken Teddy with her, leaving a hole in my life. Me not feeling the same about not seeing Heidi when I came in was proof that the relationship should've ended sooner. Two years was a good run, but in the end just added up to time wasted.

I went into the bedroom and tucked my .45 in the mounted holster attached to the bed frame, then stripped and headed for the shower. Maybe I should become one of those tools who wants sex and nothing more. That kind of guy doesn't even think about a commitment as serious as getting a dog with a woman.

Oh wait. I was that guy. Commitment, and the dog, had been on Heidi's agenda, not mine.

The water felt fantastic on the back of my neck as I held my head under the hot spray, letting it relax tight muscles as it sluiced down my shoulders and chest. For reasons I couldn't fathom, an image of a blue-blonde-haired girl came to mind. She was naked, the water beading on her pale, perfect breasts. My body responded instantly.

I cranked the faucet to cold.

CHAPTER 2

SERENA HANDED OFF a frothy cappuccino with extra cinnamon, wiped her hands on her apron and turned. Yes, she did that flick of the eyes, falter of the smile thing, every time she saw me. Hmm.

"Hello," I said, taking my eyes down the length of her pink shirt, short blue and white striped skirt, and bare, toned thighs. Down to white sneakers. Back to those thighs. When she didn't reply right away, I returned my gaze to her face. "Busy morning, huh?"

Her hair hung loose today, held away from her face by a neon green headband, and shining around her like a mane. Her look spoke of a lighthearted wildness that I was curious to see if she actually possessed.

"Uh, yes," she said, after a lengthy hesitation. "Crazy, as always. What can I get you?"

"You."

At least three patrons stopped what they were doing and stared. Serena, too.

"What time do you get out of here?" I asked.

She looked like she wanted to answer, though remained silent.

"Four? Five?"

"T—" She cleared her throat. "Two."

Her worried expression told me she already regretted answering. I'd been described as intimidating. Was that it? I smiled, and her expression went from worried to stunned. It was almost amusing to watch as her gaze focused on my mouth, then my eyes, which people had informed me could be cold. I crinkled them a little to make me look ... I don't know ... friendly?

"Should I pick you up here?"

"Uh...."

"I'd like to talk."

"Uh...." Serena blinked, but didn't respond until a co-worker elbowed her in the back. "Yeah. Sure."

She was a sweet thing, wasn't she? I had no business being interested in her. But I was. I thought of giving her my number so she could call and cancel if there was a change of plans, but I knew she'd get cold feet and use it to avoid me. I didn't want that to happen, so I took my coffee and walked out. If she was going to cancel on me, it would be at two o'clock, face to face.

I COULDN'T CONCENTRATE on anything and even Joy pretending to be nice to me didn't register long enough to get on my nerves. I didn't care about any of that right now, not her using me, or camping, or my mother, who said she had to talk to me about something serious when I got home. *Frosty* was coming for me. At two o'clock.

For some reason, I felt as though I was facing off with a bully after school. My stomach was in knots and everyone around me kept giving me sly glances. My eyes returned to the clock for at least the hundredth time today. One fifty-four. I looked out the large-paned front window.

"Yeah, he's here," Eddie said. "He's been sitting out there watching the place. Kinda creepy, if you ask me."

"Well, I didn't ask you," I snapped, immediately regretting it. "Sorry."

Eddie shrugged and moved on to the next customer.

My nerves were taut as Angelina Jolie's cheeks. Now what? Why had I agreed to meet him? I didn't even know his name, and the one we'd collectively given him didn't speak of a warm, friendly person. What was I going to do with him? And worse, what was he planning to do with me?

I was inexperienced, yes, but not as naïve as some would think. The way he looked at me didn't say, *"let's be friends."* He found me attractive, and he definitely had to know I returned his interest. But I never intended to test my interest close up. Why else would I still be a virgin at twenty-four-years-old?

Like most timid, introverted girls, I'd spent my early years swooning over TV stars and singers, and drooling over real men from afar. And while there had been some awkward groping and sloppy kisses with real boys, they had always been the ones to make the moves. Honestly, I would have been good if they hadn't. I knew girls got steamed up and hot, and wanted ... more ... but I'd never personally experienced it to the degree I believe they have. That was why I read romance novels. To *experience* such things without experiencing such things.

I watched as my *date* got out of the car and leaned against the front fender. Today he wore jeans and a long sleeve blue shirt pushed halfway up his forearms. What a body. I gave myself a mental shake. Ogling him wasn't helping.

Shoring up my courage as my co-workers teased me, I walked out the door, chin up, heart pounding mercilessly in my breast. On the plus side, everyone here knew I was going out with him and would have no problem identifying him in a line-up.

He pushed off the car as I neared. "I won't hurt you, Serena," he said, reading my mind.

The sound of his voice was like a warm caress down my soul, and it was the most bizarre thing, but I felt like I wanted to arch under the pleasure, right here in the parking lot. It was far too exaggerated a reaction for a simple sentence. It was crazy!

He smiled and scattered what remained of my senses. In self-defense, I looked down into my bag to search for some imaginary object, a diversion to avoid meeting his eyes.

"You know, I'm not going to tie you up and have my way with you," he said, causing my head to pop up. "Unless you want me to," he added.

His tone was serious, though after a of couple seconds, he smirked. "I'm kidding."

He met me at the front of the car and walked me to the passenger door, hesitating before pulling it open.

"I have a feeling you're afraid of me." He leaned in a little. "I mean, I hope you don't feel I pressured you into coming out with me."

Rather than deny it, I shrugged. He sighed.

"I don't even know your name," I said, looking up at him. He was bigger than I remembered. Six-one or two. And ... big! Like ... Thor! Okay, I may have exaggerated.

"Marcus."

Marcus. Of course it was. Marcus was a jock's name. The name of the Strongest Man in the World. The real name of a guy hiding a superhero identity.

The name of a guy who'd single-handedly saved his entire unit in a war. No guy with an inferiority complex and bad skin was ever named Marcus.

He opened my door but rested his folded hands on top of it instead of hurrying me inside.

"Take out your phone," he said.

"My phone?" When he didn't reply, I did as he asked.

"Text this to someone who will know what to do with it, should the need arise," he scoffed, but then shook his head. "Which it won't."

So, he thought I was being foolish. I rolled my eyes and moved to put my phone back.

"I'm serious," he said. "It'll give you peace of mind and I don't want you worrying I'm going to rape and murder you and stuff you in a suitcase."

I chuckled at the absurdity, but not in the way where it was humorously absurd, the way where it was too absurd to not have some kind of verbal reaction, and screaming would just be too obvious and offensive. But when he didn't smile, I clicked on my manager, Bill's, number.

"Fine. Go ahead."

"My full name is Marcus Armatura, no middle name. I'm thirty-one."

He waited while I typed. This was humiliating and I could barely text his words with my head full of my own, like *any second he's going to say "screw you", get in his car and drive away fast.* But he didn't.

"I live in Hampton County, one-fifteen Meadowlark Road, Newburg."

He gave me his phone number—twice—then leaned back from the door.

"I have a brother, David, who lives in Canada and works for a film company. And a sister, Annabella, who lives in London and works for a bank. My parents, Alfonso and Marina, are both dead, God rest their souls."

I typed furiously, *autocorrect* changing many of my intended words, and looked at him.

"That's probably more than enough for the authorities to go on," he said. "Still want to get in?"

I nodded.

"Now, hit Send before I close the door."

I did, and folded the phone in my lap as he walked around to the driver's side, the way he moved reminding me of a heavy-weight boxer heading for the ring, determined, confident, and maybe a little cocky. He could very well be a fighter, for all I knew. Before he got in, I reminded myself to breathe. I felt a little better.

No sooner had he closed himself inside with me than the words spewed out of my mouth. "You look like you're really put together. I mean, well-built, like you must do something physical. What do you do? We always wonder when you come in."

"What do *you* think I do?"

I raised my chin, eying him with a downward tilt of my head. "Boxer?"

"No."

"Mafia?"

He didn't laugh. "No."

"Hmm. Those were the only guesses I had."

"What do *they* think I do?" he asked, lifting his chin toward the coffee shop and the faces lined up in the front window.

He seemed genuinely curious, but what if it embarrassed him? Though that would take some of the focus off me, wouldn't it?

"Now that I think of it, they're all pretty much along the mafia line. *Collector*," I said, using my fingers for quotes. "You know, professional knee-breaker. Someone said hitman, outright." I placed my fingertips on my chest. "Not me. I wouldn't say that."

"Well, I try not to kill people anymore. Now I keep them alive." He smirked. "I do private security."

"Oh." I nodded. That could mean a lot of things. "Is it dangerous?"

A glint of amusement lit his eyes. "You like dangerous men, Serena?"

"No! I mean ... who ... no.... *They* say that," I said, pointing to the shop. *Nice save, Serena.* Was it possible to embarrass myself anymore? The way he was looking at me made me wonder if he already considered me weird. Or at the very least, immature.

After a moment, he laughed. It was a fabulous sound that reached inside and tickled various spots.

"You can trust me," he said. "I won't hurt you."

"Of course I can. Why wouldn't I? Obviously, I can trust you. I wouldn't be here if I thought you'd hurt me. I mean, I'd never think that."

Marcus touched a hand to my arm, interrupting my inane babbling.

"I see you're uncomfortable. And it would be easy to say this might be a mistake, and suggest we try getting together another day when you've had more time to prepare." He started the car. "But I'm not going to do that."

Marcus put the car in gear and pulled away as my phone signaled a text. Bill, asking if I was alright. I replied with a YES and smile face, but time would tell if it was the truth.

Though in time I could be dead. Everyone would know who'd done it, but I'd still be just as dead.

I tried to keep my sigh as silent as I could. Why was I here? I found Marcus attractive, everyone did, but never imagined he'd even exchange words with me that weren't order related, and now here I was in his car, with him driving me ... some place. Still, I had to say I was doing better than I'd thought I would. My words weren't sticking in my throat and I hadn't passed out yet. Go me!

"Where are we going?"

"To perform an experiment," he answered, as he made a right out of the lot without making eye contact.

Okay, maybe I'd been premature. An image in *sepia* exploded in my brain, of me tied naked to a steel medical table in a damp cellar, rusty instruments of torture spread around, a bare bulb light fixture swinging overhead.

"W—What kind of experiment?"

He did glance over then, and smirked, but didn't reply. My mind raced as I looked out the window with new purpose, memorizing every turn, every street sign. If he was going to take me somewhere and do barbaric things to me—

I caught myself then. My mind was running away with crazy ideas, with things that only happened in NCIS episodes, not real life, and certainly not mine. Although, I reminded myself, they often based those shows on genuine cases.

"You don't plan to do anything stupid, right?" he asked.

Now, that was exactly the question a killer would ask a victim. I turned to face him, leaning my body as far away into the door's armrest as it would go.

"Like what?"

"Like run."

Oh God. He wouldn't be warning me not to run if he wasn't going to take me somewhere and do dreadful things to me. I had to make a break for it. As soon as we slowed down—

"You look like you're going to bolt," he said.

"What?" I had to keep him calm, not let him know what I was up to. My only hope for escape was surprise. "Why would I do that?"

"I don't know, but the way you're gripping that door, looks like you're waiting for the right time to jump out."

"That's ridiculous." I loosened my grip and tried a diverting smile, but it felt tight and lopsided. His brows drew together when he looked at me again.

"I hope so," he said. "I don't recommend jumping out of a moving car. It's messier and hurts more than people think."

When I didn't answer, he checked his side-view mirror and moved into the right lane, clicking the blinker on as we approached the intersection.

"I guess I'll just have to take you back. I mean, if you're going to freak out."

I really was being silly, wasn't I? Predators never offered to let someone go because they were nervous, did they?

"No. I'm okay," I blurted, not knowing if that was true or not. He looked like he didn't believe me any more than I did. I touched a hand to his arm. "I'm ... overreacting. I guess. You make me nervous."

"Good."

Oh, man, what had I gotten myself into?

CHAPTER 3

I WANTED HER NERVOUS. I wanted her uptight, on edge. All the things I was in that moment, though no one would ever guess it. And I didn't understand it. Nor did I know why I'd wanted to meet her. Probably to torture myself with this sweet young thing's proximity and tantalizing scent. I could practically smell the innocence on her. Not that she was a virgin—at twenty-four and looking like that, it was highly unlikely—but she definitely had a pure quality that stirred my blood.

Now that I had met her, I'd developed this ... curiosity about her, and how much of this strange attraction was I supposed to take without making a move? Yes, it had been a while since I'd had sex, and if Serena offered, I certainly wouldn't refuse, but I expected nothing from her. My *experiment* was really about satisfying that curiosity, not my lust. I wanted to know where the line was. The one she wouldn't let me cross. I'd been seducing women a long time and in private that line was always moveable. It never took much. But how far would *Serena* let me go?

Part of it was boredom, and I guess the rest was ... yeah, to torture myself.

It was a dick move, I know, and none of my business. Here she was, bewildered and not totally trusting, and here I was hoping she wouldn't let me get under her skirt, as much as hoping she would. My eyes slid to the length of creamy thighs disappearing beneath that blue and white fabric. I clamped my jaw tight and forced my eyes back to the road, in time to stop at the sign, though a little abruptly. I really was a masochist.

To be honest with myself—and I tried to be as often as I could—there was more to this than a perverted curiosity, though I hadn't quite figured it all out yet. I'd always been protective of my family and friends, the men in my unit, poverty-stricken strangers in foreign lands. You name it, if there was an underdog, I would protect it. Oh yeah, and dogs.

It was probably withdrawals from a life of defending those underdogs that had manifested this strange and sudden surge of protectiveness toward Serena.

I didn't even know the girl, and this was some crazy stalker crap, but since seeing how compliant she was with her coworker, I needed to know she wasn't that way with just anyone. Especially not with someone who could hurt her. I wanted to make sure that a man couldn't take what he wanted without boundaries because she was too nice to say no. There were plenty of ways to take advantage of a young woman, especially if she was insecure and trying to get a man to *like* her.

Okay, even in my thoughts that seemed possessive.

I drove to the park a few miles east and pulled into the dirt and gravel lot. I came here once in a while to hike and think. I used to bring Teddy here. Most of the trails were novice friendly and regularly peopled with women with dogs and children, which was why I regularly avoided those trails. I already knew Serena wouldn't feel comfortable enough to walk with me in the woods, so I parked in front of the playground.

She looked at me, then back at the wooden construction of bridges, towers, stairs and walkways. Children crawled all over it, like ants on a candy bar, while the accompanying adults sat chatting on benches inside the fence.

"I thought you might like the park," I said.

Her dark brows pulled together as I reached for my door handle. She did the same and got out, standing at the side of the car as I walked around to her.

"You want to push me on the swing?" she asked, trying to joke, but sounding a little concerned.

If she were a different type of girl, I might read a provocative message in there, but I realized only then that coming to this spot might make me seem like a pedophile. I leaned against the car and pulled her to me gently. She was clearly not relaxed, but to my relief and pleasure—and equally, my displeasure—she came to me.

"What I have in mind is all grown-up stuff, I assure you," I said, and smiled, cautiously.

Her smile didn't reach her eyes, and her shoulders tensed when I slipped my hands around her slim waist in a loose band. Her gaze darted in every conceivable direction, but directly at me, reminding me of a bird on a perch, wary, ready to fly at the slightest alarm. I would not give her time to do that.

I raised one hand to her cheek, keeping the other around her as an anchor, and before she could think to react, dipped my head, covering her soft lips with mine.

Ah.

At the first sample of her, the single syllable skimmed my brain, echoing in a long internal sigh, before fading away, leaving no thought at all. I pulled back, clueless as to what effect I was having on her, but her effect on me pulled me back for a second taste.

Again, *Ah.*

The awareness of her sweet lips fitting exactly to mine was somehow familiar, though I'd never felt anything so simply perfect. Their texture and warmth, the subtle pressure as she faltered, intensely curious, but trying not to seem like she was kissing me back, was rousing me in ways I couldn't quite grasp.

I backed off once again, to look down at her, her eyes closed as she ran her tongue over her slightly parted lips, before lightly catching her bottom lip between her white, even teeth, unconsciously setting me on fire. I had no choice but to connect to that heat and kiss her again.

When I did, she let out a soft moan that crept into me, tightening my chest, my abdomen ... other areas. I'd never had a reaction like that. Never. Not once. Like being simultaneously lulled into, and shaken from, an erotic dream.

I parted her lips and slipped my tongue inside for what I intended to be a quick exploration. But the exploration almost immediately became the destination and I settled in for what might have been minutes, while her hands found their way around me to contract and slacken uncertainly at my waist.

I was aware of her bare thighs pressed to mine, and instead of letting my hands rove lower as they wanted to, slid one up into her hair, tugging her headband free and pulling her head back, exposing the long column of her throat.

The fingers of my other hand trailed the contour of her neck, where my lips longed to follow, but that meant I'd have to stop kissing these magnificent lips, and I couldn't bring myself to do that just yet.

The sound of children giggling suddenly reminded me we weren't alone. How could I have forgotten I'd picked this spot for the presence of people? Regretfully, I ended the kiss and looked down at her face, still slack in the weighty pleasure of making out, and forced myself to look away before I dove back in. I raised my head to look out past Serena, to a row of three children lining the fence, mouths bowed with laughter behind grimy fingers.

"We should go," I said, and handed her back the green headband.

Serena looked around and saw the children, smiled, and gave them a little wave. Later, I would identify that simple gesture as the moment I relinquished sole ownership of my heart, but right now I scowled down at her, shuffled her to the door and held it open. This experiment had taken a very sharp turn and I didn't know if it was a brilliant triumph or a miserable failure.

"Is something wrong?" she asked, a little flustered.

"Just a minor miscalculation," I said, and shut her inside.

THE PLAYGROUND WAS FULL of activity, but I can't say I was watching any of it, more like trying to follow the blurs of children as they passed in front of the windshield. My mind spun in this nebulous place of replaying what just happened, and of not understanding what just happened. I thought of those people who claimed to be victims of alien abduction and imagined this was how they must feel when waking up in their bed the next day.

I glanced over at Marcus, who stared ahead, his eyebrows pulled together a little like he was puzzling over something. Same as me. No one had kissed me like that in my life. Wow! He'd said he had "grown-up stuff" in mind, and that was the only way I could think of it now. A "grown-up" kiss, drawing a clear demarcation line, shoving anything that had come before into the "childhood" category.

I took a deep breath and turned to look out the side window before he saw how shaken I was. I mean, I didn't know if he could see it, but my ears felt hot and the rest of me trembly and anxious. Yet, the truth was, at the same time, I felt like I'd somehow *graduated*, and it was a bit of a rush.

A smile tugged at my lips, one I didn't let fully develop. I didn't want him to think me flippant about our kiss. No matter how I'd like to play the knowing, experienced kisser, I wasn't that at all.

But why had he stopped so suddenly? It couldn't be my breath. I prided myself on my oral hygiene and the last thing I ate was a piece of peppermint stick at work. His breath, too, was clean and fresh. Oh, the kids. Right ... the kids.

"So..." he said.

Startled, I turned to face forward and saw him watching me in my periphery. "So...."

"Are you hungry?" he asked.

"No." My stomach was in a twist. The excitement, bundled with the nerves, would make eating impossible.

I brought my hands together in prayer position on my lap and wedged my fingers down between my thighs to keep them warm. Parts of me were freezing, others overheated. I hoped I wasn't sweating under my short jacket. He stared at me as we sat for another awkward minute, then he started the car and backed out.

I couldn't take the strain of silence any more. I needed to say something. Anything! "I come here a lot," I said, looking at the bridge as we passed.

"Oh?"

"I like to read by the bridge."

He spared me one last look, then returned his attention to the space ahead of us as he pulled onto the main road. "What do you read?"

Even in this awkward moment, there it was, that tiny spike of embarrassment before I admitted my addiction. "Romance."

He said nothing. Didn't flinch or crack a smile. I thought there might have been a small sigh, but it could have been the air coming through the window. I didn't know if I should ask him if he read, or liked movies, or what he did for fun. I wasn't sure this was a date at all. If it was, it was the strangest I'd ever been on. Though I couldn't say it was a disappointment. Not with a kiss like that.

I put the window down another inch.

"Hot?" he asked, and slid me a look that raised my temperature another degree.

"Yeah, this jacket...." Wasn't heavy enough to keep a chill at bay, much less raise my temperature. The look he gave me said he knew it.

We drove back the way we had come, all the way back to the coffee shop. He parked where we had been before and sat quietly with the engine running until he looked over at me.

"I, uh...," he began. He rubbed his cheek with his palm and let out a quick breath. "I could lie and tell you I just remembered I have something else to do, but the truth is I don't know where to go from here."

"What do you mean? Like where to take me?" I asked.

"No." He shook his head. "I mean more ... *what* to do with you. I had a great time kissing you, but now.... There doesn't seem to be much point..."

The feeling started dead center of my chest. I didn't know if it was anger or humiliation, but it spread along my limbs, down through my stomach, tightening my internal organs until it felt like something was about to rupture. Was he really sitting here implying he'd wanted to use me for sex and realizing he wouldn't get it was ... done?

First, he hadn't tried very hard. Or at all. Not that it would have mattered, but it was like he was just ... giving up. As though he'd realized I wasn't worth the effort and could find what he was looking for elsewhere.

I closed my eyes briefly, hoping when I opened them, I wouldn't be so mortified. I seriously couldn't keep this guy's interest for the duration of a date? Though, to be fair, I couldn't believe I'd sparked his interest at all. Still, I thought the kiss went extremely well on his end, not only mine.

But when I opened my eyes, I was more embarrassed than before. Not only was he still there, looking at me like some kind of pitiful ... something, but Joy was standing in the coffee shop window. I saw her turn over her shoulder and say something, but I looked away before we could lock eyes. Great. Witnesses to my failed outing with Marcus. We'd only left a half hour ago.

Marcus hadn't missed Joy's appearance. He took a hard look at her before turning to me.

"They're going to talk, aren't they?" he asked, confusing me further.

"Uh...."

"What I'm saying is, I know it will look bad if I let you out now and leave."

I turned my palms up in my lap. "It doesn't matter."

Marcus gripped the steering wheel, using it to angle himself over the center console to kiss me. It wasn't as long, slow, or devastating as the kiss at the park, though the heat he'd already started, expanded. In a couple seconds my lips were alone again, but he didn't pull away.

"Get in your car and follow me," he said. "They'll think we're taking the party someplace else."

"Why would they think that? I wouldn't assume we're going someplace else. I'd think...." To be honest, I would rather they thought anything other than that I'd been rejected.

"You're saying that because you know the truth," Marcus said. "People like to make up their own scenarios in their minds. Like maybe we're going off somewhere to have sex."

"S—Sex?" I choked the word out. "They know me, and that I don't even know you. They would never think that," I said definitely, shaking my head.

"They will if I kiss you like *this* first."

He leaned in again, his hand leaving the steering wheel to capture my jaw, his thumb rubbing my bottom lip as he stared down at me. The gap between us disappeared and once again, his lips administered fire.

This was no quick peck. His mouth cruised over mine in no hurry to end the charade, taking his time sampling and putting on a grand show. At least I thought it must be a convincing display. I was convinced. My body melted into the seat and my brain began overheating, dispensing flashes of light and random images of bodies entwined.

Where those images had come from, who knew, but I was thinking this was far too much for a "car kiss." I reached up and wrapped my hand around his forearm. He responded by deepening the kiss, parting my lips with his tongue.

My hand fell away as I gave in to the sensation of being slowly dipped into a vat of warm honey, my body and limbs weighted to the seat, my thoughts muddled, all but for one clear idea: *If I'm ever going to drown, this is the way to do it.*

A moan escaped me, so small I didn't think he could have heard, but he stopped and pulled back to lock his mysterious dark gaze on my face. His chest rose and fell in perfect rhythm with mine, letting me know his breath was coming as hard and fast as my own. Knowing he was as affected made me feel better. It also shot a bolt of fire straight to my core and I shifted on the creaking leather.

Marcus licked his lips and lowered his head again, but snapped it back before making contact. He returned to his face-forward position in his seat, his fingers holding a white-knuckle grip on the wheel.

"That should do it," he said, after an extended pause, his voice gruff and curt.

Realizing he'd dismissed me, I unfastened my seatbelt and got out. Refusing to look at the faces in the window, I kept my head down and concentrated instead on getting my shaky legs to ferry me to my car.

Once inside, I fumbled with my seatbelt, starting the car, breathing. I didn't know what Marcus was up to, but it was bizarre. Unsettling. And exciting.

I followed him out of the parking lot, making the left behind him at the corner when I usually went right. Sure, my co-workers might now think I had turned tramp, but I was getting a kick out of it.

CHAPTER 4

WHEN SHE LICKED HER LIPS, I almost hit a parked car. I tore my gaze from the rearview mirror and returned it to the road where it belonged. What the hell was wrong with me? I knew the first time I kissed her that something wasn't right, and now that I'd gone back for another dose....

Minor miscalculation? I'd screwed up royally. There was no way I could see her again. Shame, too. I liked the coffee there, but allowing myself to feel this way was too risky. I didn't even know what *this way* was, but I didn't like it. It was unnerving.

I'd meant to take the reins and lead Serena on a brief sensual adventure for the sole purpose of learning how far she would follow. I don't know why it mattered to me and I don't know why I thought feeling her up and slipping my tongue down her throat was a good idea, but I'd thought it couldn't hurt.

Well, actually, I didn't put all that much thought into it. All the crap I'd told myself about protection and boredom was exactly that—crap. Oh, maybe I'd meant it before I kissed her, but now it was definitely about wanting her. She was hot, in an understated girl-next-door way, and what was wrong with wanting to be with a pretty girl or seeing how far I could get her to go?

Harmless. Two adults testing the waters. It had been a shock to find the tide turned in her favor. Instead, *I'd* become a trembling pile of need from kissing her. Kissing. In broad daylight. Outside. In a car. In the *front* seat. If she ever realized the power she had, the male of the species would be in trouble. I almost felt sorry for the poor slobs.

She was still following when I pulled to the curb and let her pull up next to me. She lowered her passenger window and leaned over.

"You're good from here, right?" I asked.

She blinked at me, then smiled. "Sure. Thanks."

She looked like she wanted to say something else, but the situation was already so strange, what could she say? She would go her way, I'd go mine, and never again would we meet.

I took a last long look at her blue-blonde hair, wide blue eyes, small nose, perfect, supple mouth.... I tipped my head and drove off, watching in the mirror until she made a right and disappeared.

I wish I could say I felt relief, but I could only imagine the rejection and confusion she must be experiencing. I hadn't meant for that to happen. None of this. And not seeing her again wouldn't change the fact that she had rocked me.

While it would have been fantastic to take Serena home and explore every inch of her body, I'd found an abnormal fascination and satisfaction in her kisses alone.

So much for my experiment. Sure, I could melt her using only my lips, but she could do the same to me. I had to laugh out loud. Lesson learned.

By the time I was ready to head out to escort a client to the airport, I'd convinced myself I'd overreacted. That I couldn't stop thinking about Serena because I'd left things too open-ended. I'd flat out rejected her with no excuse, and that wasn't like me at all.

By the time I watched the client's plane lift off, I couldn't help thinking that if Teddy was at home to greet me, this coffee shop girl fixation might already be spent. It was clearly a case of me looking for a little affection. Also not like me, but saying that was better than considering the alternative.

By the time I was heading home, I'd decided it was definitely the rejection thing. It wasn't fair of me to use her for my curiosity and then carelessly toss her aside.

On top of that, I'd put her in a position of being humiliated in front of her friends, or at the very least, gossiped about. I owed her an explanation. And I planned to come up with one on the way to her house.

My background made finding Serena simple, and I parked at the curb behind her car in front of her small yellow house. But so far, the only explanation I had come up with was lame. *You're hot and I was curious whether you'd let me....*

That was crazy. Especially when I had no choice but to follow it with, *I'm not rejecting you, but I don't want to see you again.* What the hell was that? Then again, I wouldn't have to worry about not seeing her, since after hearing that, she would be sure to have me banned from the coffee shop. Maybe it would be best to leave things as they were.

I was about to pull away when a beat-up red compact tooled into the driveway. A slender woman climbed—well, stumbled—out and made her way up the front steps, dropping her keys three times before finding the door lock. I opened my passenger window the rest of the way and a few seconds later heard yelling coming from inside the house. A woman—possibly the one who'd just gone inside—was ranting about dog puke. Then Serena's voice, rising and falling, not hysterical like the other, but insistent.

Something shattered inside and I was out of the car like a bullet, poised to push the front door open when it wrenched from my grasp. Serena stood trembling in the doorway dressed in gray sweatpants and a black hoodie, no shoes, and tears in her eyes.

"Marcus!"

"Are you okay?" I asked.

"And don't come back until you decide to take living here a little more seriously!" the woman yelled from somewhere out of sight.

Serena shook her head, sniffed, and ran past me and down the steps.

"You can't find a home anywh—" the woman said, halting her inebriated slur when she marched into the room and saw me. "Who are you? What do you want?"

I didn't know what to say, so said nothing.

"I asked who you were."

Now that she was closer, I could see the relation to Serena. Mother, most likely. She smelled like gin, her hair was brassy, not natural golden honey like her daughter's, and shot out in all directions. Her knee was scraped and bleeding below a much too short for her age orange skirt. She eyed me up and down, then offered me a surprisingly pleasant smile.

"You're not a detective."

"No, I'm not." As if a detective could afford this suit. Strange, though, that official business would be her first thought. "I wanted to talk to Serena."

Her spine snapped straight, and she fixed her hands on her narrow hips. "What do you want with her? You're not a friend of hers."

I wouldn't make things worse for Serena by telling this woman to mind her own damn business, but I needed to diffuse the situation.

"I am, actually." I held out my hand and smiled, expecting her to snarl or slap it away or something, but she took it, turning her head to the side to inspect me through one narrowing eye.

She held onto my hand a little longer, then dropped it and lifted her chin. "Are you dating? You and Serena? You look a little old. For *my daughter*, I mean."

Her emphasis on *my daughter* left no doubt she thought me the perfect age for her. "Not exactly," I told her truthfully.

"What's that mean, *not exactly*? You're not having sex with her."

"No, I'm not," I said, trying to keep my temper from rising.

She thought for a few seconds, then shrugged. "Well, you can see she's not here. Ran off." She leaned past me, her gin breath swiping a foul path under my nose as she leaned out the front doorway, to yell, "What can you expect from a girl who doesn't respect her mother?" She stepped back, then thought of something else that needed saying, and leaned back out. "And who can't do a few simple things around here to make my life easier!"

This time when she came back in, she grabbed hold of the door to give her sentence some punctuation, but I blocked it before it slammed. I didn't want to be closed alone inside with her for even a second.

"Okay, I'm going to go—"

"I suffer from anxiety," her mother said, looking up at me with a sparkle of tears.

It was weird, but even though I knew she'd manufactured them, I almost felt sorry for her. She looked much like Serena had moments ago.

"I've always been an anxious person," she said.

"Uh … sorry to hear that," I said, stepping one foot over the threshold.

"They used to call it *high-strung*, back when they didn't want to recognize it as an actual condition. I'm on medication for it."

"Mm hmm." Yeah, I could see that. Self-medicating as well. "Nice to meet you."

I turned and jogged down the stairs before she could say another word. The door closed none too gently behind me. Serena's car was still there, but the sidewalks and street were empty.

"Serena."

No answer. Where could she have gone? It was cold, and she didn't even have shoes. I called out several more times, walking around the house. Nothing. I got in my car and rolled down the street, scanning both sides for her. It took less than a minute for me to find her sitting on the steps of a house several doors down.

"Hey," I called out the passenger window.

Serena wrapped her arms more tightly around herself but made no move to come to me, so I put the car in park in the middle of the street and went to her, keeping my voice low since it was after one a.m. and the house was dark.

"You okay?"

"Fine." She sniffed, but kept her head lowered. Just as well. I didn't want to see any more tears.

"You don't seem fine."

"I...." She tossed her hands up and let them fall. "It's nothing new. I just can't believe you had to be there to see that. My mother...."

I held a hand out to her. "Come on." She looked up at me with miserable eyes, and I wanted to scoop her up and carry her.

"Where?" she asked.

"In the car, it's cold out here."

Finally, she stood, ignoring my hand, but I didn't read anything into that. Inside the car, I closed the windows and cranked up the heat.

"Next time you're going to storm out, you should at least have flip-flops. Something."

"Well, I didn't plan it. She woke me out of a sound sleep. I didn't know the dog threw up or I would've cleaned it."

"That's why she exploded?"

Serena nodded. "Tilda—our dog—is having some digestive issues the last few days. She ran out of food and I've been giving her whatever I can scrounge up. Not good for a dog. She's older...."

"Or a person," I said. "Have you been eating?"

"Oh, yeah. Of course."

I doubted that, and as slight as she was, she couldn't afford to lose any weight.

"But everything was fine when I went to bed."

"What does your mother do?" I asked. Couldn't wait to hear this.

"Um, she used to be an insurance agent."

"Used to be?"

"Yeah, car insurance. Now she's on disability for anxiety. And OCD. She's working part time at a dollar store somewhere."

I could tell how embarrassed she was, but whether she knew the exact truth or was in denial, she needed to hear it out loud. I hadn't missed the jaundice or the white spots dotting her mother's skin.

"She's an alcoholic, you know that."

Rather than get upset, Serena nodded. "And addicted to Xanax."

Wonderful. The woman might not last the next year.

She sat quietly and brushed a tear away with her sleeve. "I should—"

"You were sleeping?" I cut her off, not wanting her to end our time together so soon. She nodded. "In that?" I asked, giving the shoulder of her hoodie a little tug. When she didn't speak, I got the picture. "You have no heat, do you?" I'd noticed the chill in there.

Serena let out a discouraged sigh. "I should go. She probably passed out by now. She'll forget all about it by the time she wakes up."

Yes, it was time to let her go. The longer I kept her here, the more I learned about her, and it only drew me closer. There was that protective thing again. I drove her back to the house and watched her walk up the steps, hoping her mother hadn't locked the door and had indeed passed out. Serena opened the door and disappeared into the dark interior without looking back.

CHAPTER 5

"WELL?"

I glanced into my manager's curious eyes. "Well, what?"

"The date. *Frosty*. What happened?"

"Well, he didn't cut me up into bite-size chunks," I joked. Though Marcus had nearly devoured me at the park, and again in the car. And *again* in the car, I remembered with a flush.

"I mean, if you want your affairs kept private, you shouldn't make out in front of the place you work," Bill said with a chuckle.

I laughed, too, though I wondered if everyone here had indeed assumed I went home with Marcus. Considering that brought its own measure of distress, but it was better than reliving the horrendous display put on by my mother when he showed up. The humiliation, the disappointment. Now he knew I lived with a drug-addicted alcoholic in a house without heat. If I never saw him again, it wouldn't be long enough for the mortification to wear off.

Fortunately, I didn't see him all day. After three months, he must know I rarely work on Fridays and had forgotten I was covering for Joy while she enjoyed her day off.

Propping my elbows on the counter, I dropped my chin in my hands. I should be out in the woods gathering kindling for a fire later. I should be laughing with friends and hiking through brightly colored foliage and praying to God we didn't run into a bear. Instead, I was here, filling drink orders for snooty lacrosse moms and teen girls trying to grow up too fast.

That had been me, so long ago it seemed. It almost made me laugh. Going for coffee with friends was the definition of adulthood back then. Bye-bye sugary sodas—at least when friends were around—and hello to dark brewed beverages we couldn't pronounce, much less swallow without wincing. We got used to them, though, that's what grown-ups do. They get used to things.

All kinds of things, like being controlled and mistreated, like my mother had. Then she'd gotten used to waiting for my father to come back to our tiny dilapidated house with the busted boiler and shredded roof. Sometimes people got used to things never changing.

I can't let that be me. Not like her. It's why I keep pressing on, taking every job I can manage, so one day soon I can step up out of that hole and move forward.

I think my mom wants me gone, anyway. She's been saying she wants to talk to me, but then gets wasted and we fight, so maybe it's something hard to talk about. Like her moving in her boyfriend, Tank. No, I'm not kidding. Tank. That's the only name I've ever heard him called. She knows I can't stand the guy and that living under the same roof would be unbearable.

Me not dating much seems more of an annoyance to her than a relief. It's like she wants me to get out there and get my heart stomped, so I'll understand what she went through with my father. No, she's never said so. It's only a thought. One of the dark ones I allow myself when I'm too exhausted to be optimistic and cheery. Sheesh, some days I make myself gag.

The door opened with a gush of cold air, and I looked over expectantly. But it wasn't Marcus. I quickly squelched the nudge of disappointment in my stomach by returning my thoughts to my friends and my missed camping trip.

THE DOOR OPENED SEVERAL hundred more times between then and Wednesday, and not one of those times was it to let Marcus in. I'd given up wondering how he had found where I live. He said he did private security so I guess there were many avenues to locate me, but I had given up thinking he'd ever find his way back to the house, or my job.

Whatever misguided sparks our strange meetings seemed to ignite were out now, and who could blame him? My life was a mess. I was a poor girl living in an icy hovel with a mother who was a junkie and an embarrassment. A man like that didn't need to slum it, copping a few kisses from a girl like me.

The strange thing was the time we'd spent together didn't collectively add up to more than an hour and a half. Why did it feel like I'd known him so much longer? I shot a look down at the romance novel on my car seat. That could be one reason. He embodied so many of the fictional heroes I read about. Gorgeous, intense, mysterious.... Or maybe that he occupied my thoughts almost entirely. I'd never had this happen before, like a burr in my brain.

After a quick trip to the supermarket on the way home from work, I started backing out of the diagonal space when a car stopped behind me. Dead behind me. I beeped, but it didn't move. My rearview was too small to get a good look, so I turned as far as I could in the seat. The black BMW wasn't familiar. The driver, however, was. Marcus looked me in the eye, gestured for me to follow, and pulled away.

I would have to be nuts to follow him, right? Was I nuts? I asked myself this very question as I drove behind him out of the lot for a few miles in the opposite direction of my house. It wasn't until we passed the coffee shop that I knew where we were heading.

We pulled into the park's unpaved lot, by the bridge this time. It was a gusty day, rain probable at any moment and the lot was empty except for us. I stopped in the middle, not wanting to commit to getting out. Marcus circled me and pulled up next to my door, facing the opposite way.

"What's up?" I asked, trying to sound unshaken by him or the fact that he'd somehow willfully abducted me. That was how it felt. Like I wanted to come here, but hadn't actually had a say in it.

He didn't answer for a long time, only stared. Long enough for me to wonder if this was some kind of set-up, and any minute my car was going to be besieged by cammo-clad soldiers.

"I was in the neighborhood," he said, finally.

"Seriously?" I asked. His lips quirked. "Why did you bring me here?"

"I didn't. You followed me. You didn't have to."

"You knew I would."

His faint smile smoothed to a grim line, and his forehead furrowed. "Yes."

"And that annoys you," I said. I saw it now. The same as I had the day with Joy at All You Can Brew. This wasn't a set-up, it was a test, and apparently, I'd failed, given him what he'd expected. Compliance. All I could do was shake my head.

That, and drive away.

I had gone about fifty-feet when he deliberately backed his car in front of mine, making me slam on my brakes.

"What's wrong with you?!" I yelled out my window.

"I want to talk to you."

"Well, I don't want to talk to you!"

I reversed and pulled away. Again, he blocked me.

"I can do this all day, sweetheart," he said.

I knew he would. We'd drive in short spurts around and around this lot looking like a couple of idiots. There was no fear, but my frustration was beyond words right now, and with it an anger I couldn't explain.

First of all, I didn't like feeling trapped. Never had. I wasn't claustrophobic, but I wanted to know that I could leave if I wanted to. Apart from that, I was genuinely mad at him. Sure, it was his prerogative not to like my passive nature, but then why bother with me at all?

"Leave me alone," I said.

"I'm trying to."

His answer made no sense. Was he on drugs? Was everyone but me on some mind-altering chemical?

"I'll make it easy for you. Get out of my way."

"We need to talk first," he said.

"About what? How stupid I am to follow you here when I should have stood up for myself and said screw you? Well, I'm doing it now. Screw you!"

He looked down at his floor, dissatisfaction plain on his face. Like I was a disrespectful child he tolerated, and his patience was growing thin.

"Serena, I was working."

The sentence threw me, partly because it had come out of nowhere, partly because he sounded like he was explaining himself. To me. Why?

"What? What are you talking about?"

"I haven't been around because I've been working. Out of town. You must have wondered where I was."

I wish I could've said he sounded conceited about it, but he didn't. Just matter-of-fact. It was the logical assumption.

"I get that you're mad," he said.

"You get...." Then what he was saying caught up with my brain. "Wait, is that what you think? That I'm mad because you didn't keep in touch?"

His look told me that was just what he'd thought.

"And for rejecting you the other day. That's what I want to talk to you about."

"You don't owe me an explanation."

Marcus got out of his car and tugged on my door handle.

"What are you doing?" I asked.

Before I could get frightened or defensive, he reached in, clicked the unlock button, and had me out of the car. Closing the door, he stood me in front of him, spreading his stance and pressing my butt against the car.

In reply to my question, he kissed me. Hard, gentle, I had no idea. I couldn't feel his lips directly, only the liquid fire that poured into my body, doing its best to melt me into a puddle at his feet. He finished way too soon for my liking, and I found myself trying to clear my vision as I looked up into his amused, dark eyes.

His fingers were firm around my upper arms, his thumbs rubbing back and forth. "Why don't you tell me why you're angry?"

Angry? Who was angry? Anger was impossible with this warm drug coursing through my veins. I looked at him from beneath heavy lids. The worst I could manage was mild annoyance.

But when he smirked, the drug dissipated and I remembered why I was annoyed. I blew out a frustrated breath.

"Really?" I asked. He stopped rubbing and looked at me, questioning. "Asking me to follow you and then acting like you're disappointed that I did? Like I'm some stupid girl, doing what I'm told?"

He tightened his grip. "I don't think you're stupid, Serena. That's what drives me crazy. I can see you're smart, intelligent, but you have an over-developed sense of ... nice, that can get you into trouble."

"So, I shouldn't be nice? Maybe I should be more like you, just use people." He didn't reply, which confirmed what I'd thought, that he wanted a *dolly* to play with and mold, that was all. "And who are you to approve or disapprove, anyway? What I do and who with is none of your business."

Wow, I couldn't believe I said that. I never told people off!

His left eye narrowed a little and a scene from CSI flashed through my mind, where a raging guy kills and buries a girl in the woods because she speaks up instead of just keeping her mouth shut. Yet with my adrenaline already pumping, I went on.

"I know you were only trying to get me into bed, but you lost interest when you found out I don't have enough backbone for you." He opened his mouth to speak, but I talked right over him. "And why did you kiss me now? To torture me? Or see if you could make my knees weak?"

"Serena—"

"I don't know what you want, maybe a girl who plays hard to get and teases you, or an aggressive one who sticks her tongue down your throat, I don't know, but I'm obviously not good enough for you.... Especially after seeing how I live."

"Serena—"

"And that's fine," I said, holding a hand up in a stop gesture. "I get all that. But I'm not letting someone—especially a guy who only wants me for entertainment—try to make me something I'm not." My bottom lip threatened to quiver then. I pressed my lips together, lifted my chin and looked him in the eye. "I may be a pushover with some people, but I do know how to say no."

He didn't answer, but then what could he say? I'd nailed it. He knew it, I knew it.

His eyes widened briefly, and he released my arm and stepped back. "I can't believe this," he said, irritated. As if he was somehow insulted. "You really think that? That I don't want you because you're too compliant?"

I didn't know what to say.

"Yeah, I rejected you the last time we were together here, but not for any reason you think. That's why I came to your house, to—"

"Why *did* you come to my house?" I asked. "Not to sleep with me?"

"To do what I'm trying to do now, if you'd let me get a word in!" He gritted his teeth, frustration clear in his voice, and the way his hands balled then loosened. He raked a hand over his face and leaned next to me on the car, crossing his arms over his chest.

"YOU WANT THE BLUNT TRUTH? No games?" I asked her. She nodded. "I do want to have sex with you, Serena. I do, and I don't care if it's in a bed, or the car, or here, up against a tree, or if I'm not supposed to say it to you. It's true and now you know it."

Her eyes widened. More than that, I could see the pulse beat at the base of her throat. Her heart was suddenly pounding, her breath coming faster, and I would bet almost anything it wasn't from fear. I tried to ignore my own reaction to that.

"But it's not because you're a mark. It's because I find you sexy and interesting."

"What?"

Her eyes widened further, and she tilted her head, genuinely surprised. Had no one told her that before?

"Do you remember the first time I saw you?" She shook her head. No, how would she know the first time I'd seen her? "Your hair was reddish ... shorter than now, and you were wearing cut-off shorts and a yellow T-shirt under your apron. And when you climbed that little stepstool to get something...." I blew out a breath and shook my head. I'd done it then, too.

She narrowed her eyes. Either she thought I was lying now, or couldn't believe I'd thought of her that way even then, but it was true, if only partly. The whole truth was once I'd seen her smile, and how she treated people, I was hooked. I couldn't tell her that. I hadn't even admitted it to myself until this very minute. Though *hooked* might be too strong a word. *Intrigued to the point of distraction*, maybe.

She cleared her throat. "Well, it was July. It was hot," she said, letting me know she was conscious of exactly how long I'd been around.

"Yes, it was."

She shook her head. "W—Why didn't you ever say anything to me?"

My lips curved at the corners. "I was biding my time until I had something to say."

She stiffened then. "And the first thing you said was basically that I'm an idiot."

"I never said that."

She nodded. The *yeah, whatever* kind.

"And today you did it again," she said.

I wanted to argue, but she was right, wasn't she?

"I'm sorry. I didn't mean it to come across that way. I'm only trying to...." What? I didn't know any more. I don't know if I ever knew. "No more games," I promised her. "The fact of the matter is I wasn't sure I should get involved with someone as nice as you." I held a hand up. "And before you get defensive, I don't mean that as a criticism. I mean, you're the type of girl who's looking for more than a quick tumble, and I can't promise you more than that."

"But you asked me out anyway," she said, her voice full of accusation, taking me to task again.

She was tougher than I'd given her credit for. She lowered her eyes, but I ducked my head to meet them and bring her gaze back to mine.

"Right. And now that I have...."

I leaned in slowly to kiss her, but she leaned back.

"Now that you have, what? You got a little taste, and now you think you're going to get the whole plate? Maybe I don't want you," she said.

Okay, she was still mad. And to my detriment, I was sure, I found this side of her incredibly arousing. I tried to slip my arms around her waist, but she pulled away.

"Are you mentally ill?" she asked, quite serious.

It was a legitimate question. One I'd been asked before under different circumstances. "I must be," I said, taking her hand.

"Stop it," she said, tugging it, but I didn't let go.

Though maybe it was lust, pure and simple, that had me acting this way, and once slaked, I could go back to being myself. I shook my head to dislodge an image of us entwined in the back seat, and ignored the temptation to run my hands down her hips and around to her luscious derriere, firm and rounded just the way I like it.

I told myself it was for her benefit, that I didn't want to scare her away, but I knew the truth as I stood there swinging her hand slowly, awkwardly, back and forth while I tried to figure out what to do in this moment.

If I didn't know better, I'd think I was falling for her, which was utterly ridiculous. Utterly. Before our first kiss six days ago—which should never have happened the way it did—she was just a cute barista who avoided eye contact. Since then, she occupied more of my thoughts than she should. *Too much too soon...*

After a really lengthy, uncomfortable minute of silence, I let go of her hand and stepped back.

"I'll see you later."

Her non-committal shrug made me smile, but the dazed expression that went along with it gave me pause and had me wondering if I was as crazy as she obviously thought I was. As I watched her get in her car and drive off, that smile vanished completely. Crazy or not, I was in over my head.

CHAPTER 6

MY GAZE SNAPPED BACK to the living room window. Habit now, after seeing Marcus' car drive by as soon as I got home. It was like he'd beaten me here and had been waiting to see I made it home. It was strange. A little sweet, but after what happened at the park, a little stalkery, too.

I still couldn't wrap my mind around what had gone on. He had made little sense about why he'd come for me, or the things he said when we got to the park. He was smug, but at the same time a little unsure. It was weird. Had to be drugs. Or mental illness.

My Aunt Cissy was a clinical psychologist, and I was seriously considering asking for her advice. First, she could give me a quick rundown of his diagnosis, then she could tell me why I was so screwed up that I followed him into an empty park. And why I thought about him since we met.

He was definitely strange. Stranger yet was the notion of him *desiring* me. There were, of course, times I'd wanted boys to notice me, or think me cute, or smart, even a little sexy, but once again, that was back in my *childhood* mindset, before Marcus had erased all that with one kiss. Now he'd forced me to admit I wanted to be desired. By him.

I felt the color crawl up my face once again. Earlier, when I was indulging in a brief fantasy of Marcus and I steaming up the car windows in that parking lot, my mother had seen me blush and felt my head for fever. I was definitely warm, but I'd told her I'd exerted myself reaching under the couch for a wayward sock.

I went back to my chores and didn't notice him drive past again. It was just as well. All this thinking about him was stressing me out, and on top of it, my mother started drinking earlier than usual after coming in from God knew where. She'd been on the phone in her bedroom with the door closed, her voice lowered like she didn't want me to hear. Now she was pacing the house, picking up flecks of dirt. A sure sign her OCD was flaring up.

I knew what was coming. First the questions: *"Did you scrub the trash can before you put a new bag in?" "How many times do I have to ask you to throw out the butter when there's only this tiny piece left?" "Did you refill the ketchup?"*

That last one always got me. The sound of anything coming through a squeeze bottle, making that farty, sucking sound, could send her over the edge, but she refused to buy it in glass bottles, and instead had me empty it into mason jars so she could spread it with a knife. Weird stuff.

Next there would be the cleaning of the shower curtain liner—don't even get me started on that—and then she would pick a fight with me over something equally ridiculous. I guess fighting was a way for her to relieve her stress, but it sure didn't help mine.

A knock at the door made me jump. Marcus wouldn't come here again, would he? I approached the door cautiously, because cautious was smart where Marcus was concerned, but pulled it open to find Tank standing there, a sour expression on his leathered, haggard face. It was the only expression he owned. Well, other than the one coming on now, the lecher, eying me up, down, and sideways.

"Hey there, Sabrina."

Always got my name wrong. Always.

"Hey."

I stepped back to let him in, careful not to breathe in his alcohol-soaked breath, and to keep my front toward him so he couldn't see my butt. I could almost feel it when he looked at my butt. Like insects crawling under my skin. I didn't want to be alone with him any longer than was absolutely necessary.

"I'll go get Mom," I told him, and side-stepped my way out of the room.

This would be a great time to wake Tilda from her nap in the kitchen and take her for a walk. Born deaf, she was oblivious to everything unless she felt it or was looking at it, so hadn't heard Tank come in, thankfully. Sweet as she was, the old girl was a little dopey and always toddled up to him, even though he shooed her away every time.

On the way to get my jacket from my room, I stopped by the bathroom where my mother was applying a fourth coat of mascara.

"Tank's here," I said.

"Serena, where are my gold hoops?" she asked.

"Beats me. Where'd you see them last?"

"They were in my jewelry box where they always are."

"Maybe you put them on the dresser. Or in your bag."

"You think I don't know where I put my own earrings?"

Here we go. Let the arguing commence. "I don't know, I haven't seen them."

She slammed the mascara tube on the sink edge and spun to face me, her hair flying out around her, then coming to hang half in her eyes. She shoved it back and glared at me. "Don't act like you don't know where they are."

"Mom, what are you talking about?"

"You've been stealing from me!"

I couldn't believe my ears. "What?"

"I've been missing quite a few things lately," she said. "My gold lighter, and that pen I got from the insurance company when I left."

"And you think *I'm* taking your stuff?" I could barely get the words out.

"Who else?"

"Why would I take anything from you?" I asked. "You're my mother. That's crazy."

"Oh, crazy, is it?"

"Yes. And you don't have anything I would want, anyway. Why don't you ask your boyfriend where your things have been going?"

"Oh boy, what's going on in here?" Tank asked with a snide smile on his pie-shaped face. "You ladies need to calm down."

"She's been stealing from me!" my mother ranted.

"I have not!"

"And she tried to blame you!" she accused.

"What?" Tank asked, his shocked expression exaggerated.

"Even though she says my things aren't good enough for her and she wouldn't want anything I had."

"She said that?" Tank asked her before glaring at me.

"I guess now that she's with that rich guy, she's too good for me anymore. Well, you know what? Good! At least you're saving me the trouble of asking you to move."

"Move?" I'd felt it coming, but wow, to hear it from her lips....

"Yes, Tank is moving in and I know you don't like him, so it's better for everyone if you go."

Tears stung my eyes. I couldn't believe how much that hurt.

"Not that you appreciated the roof over your head all these years," she said. "This is ridiculous!"

I turned to leave, but my mother caught me by the sleeve.

"Don't you walk away from me, Serena."

She yanked me backward, knocking me into both her and Tank in the narrow hallway.

"Don't you shove me!" my mother yelled, pulling back and wrapping her arms around herself.

"What?"

"Did you shove your mother?" Tank demanded. As if he had any right.

"I did not shove you, Mom, you pulled me into you."

She blinked, like she was trying to recall the events of only seconds ago, but Tank pushed her aside, knocking her onto the bathroom floor, and grabbed me by the arm, yanking it up behind my back with a painful twist.

"Stop!" I screamed. "What are you doing?!"

He pressed my face against the wall, his rough fingers scraping against my lower back as he tried to loosen his belt behind me.

"Sometimes a girl needs a good ass whipping, no matter how big she thinks she is," he snarled in my ear. "Learn some respect for your elders."

"Tank, let her go," my mother said, getting to her feet. He ignored her, but she jerked on his arm. "Tank, that's enough."

"This is why she is this way," he said, shaking her off. "You're too easy on her."

Pulling his belt free of the loops, he loosened his grip enough that I squeezed out from between him and the wall, shot to my room and slammed and locked the door. I had hardly enough time to fling the window up before he burst through the door, splintering wood.

"You little bitch." He took two steps toward me.

"Help!" I screamed out the window.

He froze. "Shut up!"

"Someone help!"

"Someone'll hear, then you're really going to get it," he warned, and took another step, raising the belt overhead.

I curled into the corner on the floor, closed my eyes, and covered my head with my arms, waiting for the blow. There was commotion from the hall that could have been my mother and Tank scuffling.

My mother screamed, and then a sound that chilled me to the bone.

The cocking of a gun.

Oh, God! Tank was going to shoot me right here on my bedroom floor, and probably kill my mother right after! But I couldn't open my eyes. Not until I heard the voice.

"You'll be dead before you hit the floor."

Marcus.

I opened my eyes. Marcus stood in the doorway with a gun pressed tight to Tank's head, his finger on the trigger. Tank had lost his red-faced arrogance and was peeing himself, the belt coiled loosely at his feet like a dead snake.

"Please. Please don't shoot me," Tank begged as the wet spread down his leg and all over my carpet.

"I'm having a very hard time not pulling this trigger," Marcus growled, his voice vibrating with rage. "I'm not sure I won't."

"I wasn't gonna hurt her. I wanted to scare her! That's it!"

Marcus smashed the gun into the side of Tank's face and blood spurted from a gash on his brow bone. "And what about you? Are you scared now? Are you good and scared?"

Tank's voice cracked. "Y-Yes. Yes."

"You should be. You say one more word and I'm going to put a bullet through your brain. Not another syllable, do you hear me?"

Tank nodded at lightning speed.

"Stop! I'm going to call the cops!" my mother yelled.

"Shut up," Marcus told her. "If either of you speak, I'm going to shoot you both. Not a word."

There was no inane babbling like in the movies, but a terrified squeak from my mother when Marcus hit Tank again—which I had to say I enjoyed, even in my terror.

Marcus looked at me. "Close that window."

I did, and when he gestured for me to come to him, I did that too. It was the most bizarre thing I'd ever experienced in my life, and I still didn't know whether to feel relief or horror.

"Tell me what to do," Marcus said.

"What?"

"Tell me to shoot him."

My mother gasped. Tank made a horrified squealing sound in the back of his throat, but neither of them spoke.

"I—"

"Say the word and it's done," Marcus said, his intense gaze telling me this wasn't a scare tactic. I believed wholeheartedly that if I said *shoot*, he would.

I shook my head. "No."

"Not your mother, just him."

"No."

He waited a beat. "You sure?"

"Yes." I held my breath, hoping he didn't decide to do it, anyway.

Marcus' jaw muscles flexed, and he leaned into Tank's ear. "You hear me, scumbag?"

Tank was a few inches shorter and looked up into Marcus' face and nodded vigilantly.

"This girl is kind enough to let you live. You don't deserve it. I know it and so do you. And the next time I see you, if you look at me crooked, or if I hear that you so much as breathed in Serena's direction, I'm going to kill you no matter what she says. Do you understand?"

Tank nodded and cried a little. As messed up as my mother was on pills and booze, she cried, too, and mouthed a *thank you* to me behind Marcus' back.

I didn't even know what to think. Of my mother accusing me of stealing, and Tank trying to whip me like a dog to get his jollies. Of my mother thanking me for not having him killed, when she should have been threatening to kill him herself, or demanding he get out. Or of Marcus storming in like a romance hero and saving my hide. Any of it.

"Get your things," Marcus told me.

Marcus made Tank sit in his piss, and my mother sit in the hall, while I gathered up whatever belongings I considered mine.

Five minutes later, with Tilda on her leash beside me, wagging her tail, and everything else I owned stuffed in a black trash bag, I stood there on the front porch. I had nowhere to go, no money for a place, and for all I knew, they would call police the minute we left.

Yet it was so surreal I couldn't even work up tears for my miserable predicament, or the demise of the relationship with my mother. I knew I wouldn't speak to her after this. Maybe ever again. Definitely not until she got some help.

There was no sound from inside, but when I looked through the front window, I saw Marcus speaking to my mother, his hands empty, the gun tucked away. She stood completely still, but as he walked out, she collapsed onto the sofa and cried. I turned away, not wanting to watch her shoulders and slim back rise and fall, or imagine hearing those sobs. I had no sympathy to spare. She'd ruined her life with drugs and alcohol and mental illness she never sought help for. Now she was on her own.

And so was I.

CHAPTER 7

S ERENA DIDN'T CRY.

She followed in her car to my house and seemed perfectly fine—well, maybe a little distant—but she didn't cry. I almost blew a guy's brains out all over her room and her reaction was ... minimal. She'd been threatened, abused, her mother had turned on her, and nothing. Shock. I'd seen it often enough in my career.

Even now she sat on my couch, staring at my weapon where I'd placed it on the coffee table. I didn't know if it disturbed her, or if she was only staring at that spot zoning out, but I moved the gun to the fireplace mantel where she couldn't see. When I couldn't take the suspense anymore, I sat next to her.

"Serena, are you okay?"

A bright, *'Sure! I'm great!'* would have been fantastic. She shrugged.

"I don't know how to answer that," she said quietly, still staring at the spot where my gun had rested. "How am I supposed to know?"

I thought I saw a glimmer of a tear. I was hoping for one as much as dreading it. But she held back. Her dog wandered in from her exploration of the new surroundings and sat at my feet, nudging my hand onto her tan head.

"My mother was looking for an excuse to throw me out this whole time. I knew something was up. That she wanted to move her horrible loser boyfriend in. He makes more money than I do and shares her ... interests."

Okay, so she wasn't in shock, just pissed. That was good.

"Did he ever hurt you before?" I thought I'd concealed the fury in my voice pretty well, but her eyes snapped to mine.

"No, Marcus. He was always a slimy piece of crap, leering at me...." She looked away, then back. "You would've shot him, wouldn't you?"

Her expression told me she didn't need to hear the words. She inhaled deeply through her nose and placed her palms on her thighs.

"I'm glad it didn't come to that," she said. "And I'll be out of your hair as soon as I can. It's too late to call my friend, Lisa. She'll be asleep. But I don't know what I'm going to do with Tilda," she said, reaching over to scratch the dog's chin.

"You don't have to go," I told her, rubbing Tilda's head and neck. "You can stay as long as you like."

Serena nipped her bottom lip and looked down at her feet. "I don't want to give you the wrong impression. I mean, the sleeping arrangements—"

"Are up to you," I said, harsher than I'd meant. "There's a spare room upstairs and another off the kitchen if you'd rather not be on the same floor."

"Marcus, I—"

I stopped her with a hand on her arm. "I'm sorry. I don't mean to be short. I don't want you worried I'm going to expect sex in exchange for a place to stay."

Though, she had every right to suspect that was my offer, given our previous ... *heated* interactions.

She nodded. "I'm being a little over-sensitive, I guess. Rough night."

She broke then, hands over her eyes, the tears coming so hard and fast I wasn't sure she would get her next breath in time to keep from passing out. I did the only thing I could. Hugged her tight and let her cry it out as Tilda tried to wedge between our feet, offering her own brand of comfort.

Fortunately, the torrent was fast moving, and a minute later, Serena blew her nose on a paper towel.

"I'm sorry. I don't usually do that," she said trying to smile.

"Maybe you should more often. Cathartic." I didn't know what I was saying. It sounded like something my sister would say, but I was out of my element here. "Are you hungry?" It didn't matter. She needed to eat. So did I. "Come on."

I took her hand in mine and led her to the kitchen and to the small table near the sliding doors, the dog lumbering after.

"Wow," she said, looking around. "This is the kitchen people dream about."

"Came with the house."

Her eyes were puffy and glossy, her hair a mess, there was a scrape across her right cheek from the altercation I supposed, but she was the cutest thing I'd ever seen. And tiny, I realized. Or perhaps her sudden exaggerated vulnerability made her seem so. Anyway, she wasn't over five-four.

"The guest room is right there." I pointed. "But sleep wherever you want. Tomorrow you can have my room if you want it." Her eyebrows rose slightly. "It has the best view of the hills and I won't be here. I'm leaving in the morning. I'll be gone about a week."

I watched her face as that information sank in. Did I see disappointment or only hoped I did?

"Where are you going?" she asked. "Or aren't you allowed to tell?"

"Palm Springs."

"Do you golf?"

"No. I'm working."

"Standing around looking intimidating?" she asked, smiling.

"Let's hope. Should be interesting."

My client was having a house party at his compound and there were more than a couple of shady characters on the guest list, mostly coked-up actors and porn stars. I rarely took this kind of gig, but the pay was too good to pass up this time.

"Great weather there, I hear." Her smile faded. "Have you ever had to...."

"Use force?" I asked. "Yeah, sure." But I didn't want to talk about that. "What do you want to eat?"

"You were in the military, weren't you?" she asked, evading my question.

"Six years." Then some mercenary work not worth mentioning. "Been back a few years. I'm still adjusting to home life."

"I'm not surprised it's taking so long since you're never here," she said, then dipped her chin down. "Sorry, I shouldn't have said that. It's none of my business."

"You didn't say anything wrong. It's true. But I have a job to do."

"Can't let go of keeping people safe?" she asked, smiling again.

"Old habits.... Anyway, the pay is great and I get to be home more." I tipped my head in deference to her earlier comment. "More than I used to be."

"You don't strike me as a homey kind of guy."

"I don't?"

"Not that it's a bad thing," she said. "Everyone's different, right?"

"I loved being at home as a kid." I felt a smile coming on, remembering. "I was out with my friends a lot, doing all the crazy stuff—homemade bike ramps, trying to fly off the garage roof, all that. But I liked staying in about as much. There was always a...." I shook my head. "A good vibe, if you want to call it that. Home was comfortable and...." I leaned back on my palms on the countertop.

"I don't know how to explain it without sounding like one of those guys on HGTV."

She giggled and my chest squeezed uncomfortably.

"So, you are a homebody," she said.

"Well, I was. Until my parents died."

"I'm sorry," Serena said. "Was it long ago?"

"When I was in my teens."

She gave a tiny nod. "I'm sorry, anyway."

And I was sorry to erase her gentle curve of lips.

"I remember you mentioning they had passed … in the text to my manager."

Yes, I remembered. The day I'd first kissed her.

"What about your father? Is he alive?" Serena's face changed little. No evident attachment.

"He left when I was eight. He owns a strip club outside of Miami."

"Ever see him?"

"Not once since. Not even a card."

"I'd say I was sorry, but he didn't deserve you." I wondered if I shouldn't have said that, but it was the truth. And it brought back that smile.

"You always say exactly what's on your mind, don't you?" she asked, taking a good long look at me.

"No. I don't." And it was a good thing, or right now she might be blushing.

But maybe she guessed, because in the next moment she cleared her throat and addressed the dog, talking sweetly to her, rubbing her face.

"How long have you had her?" I asked.

"Eleven years. She's deaf. I don't know if I told you that."

I shook my head, ignoring the faint tug on my heart where Teddy used to be.

"You like dogs?" she asked.

"Yeah. Used to have one, but my ex-girlfriend took him in the split."

Serena pouted. "I'm sorry. It must be hard for you. They become so important. Did you have him long?"

"Two years. But he was a little older than that. Rescue. Eh, it's just as well she got him. I'm hardly here, like I said."

"But you miss him." It wasn't a question. "I'm glad. It's good to know you feel that strongly about someone."

Her eyes warmed and sparkled and I suddenly wanted to kiss her brainless. Instead, I cleared my throat. "Yeah, well, if I felt the same about the girl, I wouldn't be missing Teddy."

She giggled like I'd wanted her to. "That's a cute name. Her idea, I take it?"

"Mine, if you must know," I said, feigning insult. "Named after my best friend. Both been through a lot. Teddy's blind in one eye from a dog fight, I think. Ted lost an eye to a sniper."

But that wasn't a tale I would recount right now, especially after her wince. I took out my phone and made a note to call Ted tomorrow, then thought maybe I would just jog over there later for a drink. He only lived five miles from here. While I was at it, I'd ask him to check on Serena while I was away.

"Okay, back to food."

CHAPTER 8

THE DROP IN TEMPERATURE brought a steady flow of customers most of the morning, but persistent rain kept them away all afternoon, so there was nothing to do but read. Joy made that practically impossible, turning up the radio and singing every song she knew, which seemed to be all of them.

"I hate fall," she said, during a commercial break. "All the rain and bare trees. Everything's dying. What's the point?"

"Change." I came to the window and stood with her.

"What change?"

"Old leaves die so new ones can grow," I said.

"What for? They're doing the same things the old ones did, hanging around blowing in the wind. Why not keep the old ones?"

She had a point. What was the point of change if it wasn't really change at all? That had me thinking about my current situation. I'd split from my mom and was staying in Marcus' empty home for the time being, but I was the same me, working the same job. I needed a bigger change. Grander. Bolder.

I had to save harder for nursing school, though while I wasn't helping my mother out any longer, that money would now have to go toward rent and utilities somewhere else. And food. I'd still be living on Raman and microwave dinners. Nothing like the meal Marcus had bought last night. Italian, from a proper restaurant, not a pizzeria. I licked my lips and smiled just thinking about the hot spaghetti and sausage. And warm bread.

"What's on your mind?" Joy asked with a wink. "Thinking about thawing out *Frosty*?"

Heat exploded up through my cheeks and ears like an inverted waterfall. Was that what she really thought? I laughed nervously. "No."

Joy laughed. "Come on, you were hooking up right out front. And who could blame you with a guy like that?!"

"We haven't—"

"Yeah, okay...." she answered.

I shot Bill a look.

"Hey, you put on a show, have to expect some reviews," he said, laughing and backing away with hands raised. He was joking, but ... was he?

"I'm so jealous!" Joy said, hopping up on the counter. "What's he like in bed? Fantastic right?"

"I have no idea!" The sheer shock of her accusation had me laughing. Me! In bed with Marcus! Although, that had more or less been the image Marcus was trying to project that day and I had gone along with it.

Now that I thought about it, to have a man kiss me in such a way, with that much attention, passion and determination.... It was well worth any snide comments and whispered remarks behind my back. Or to my face.

I tried to ignore Joy and go back to my book, but when a customer came in, Joy made no move to help him.

"Hello, can I help you?" I asked, returning to my post at the end of the counter by the register.

"Serena?" he asked, staring at me with a gray eye, his voice deep in his broad barrel chest.

His knit cap was pulled down low to the top of a black eye patch, and although we hadn't met, I instantly identified him. I'd seen one-eyed men before, but this man had almost the same ... aura as Marcus. Watchful, tough. Dangerous.

"Yes." I reached over the counter. "You're Ted?"

He smiled and shook my hand. "I see Marcus told you about me."

There was what appeared to be burn scarring across his right cheekbone beneath the patch, and some other scars, too, but I didn't want to look too closely and embarrass him.

"That he named his dog after you, yes."

Ted winced. "That's my legacy."

I giggled. "Well, it's nice to meet you. What can I get for you?"

He ordered a latte and sat at a round table while he sipped, phone in hand. I was sure he was texting Marcus. It made me feel safe, like when Marcus had driven past my house. Though safe from what, I didn't know.

Ted stayed the remaining twenty minutes while we closed up, going outside so we could lock the door, and waiting for me to come out.

"See you tomorrow," I told Bill and Joy, who sent nods in return.

"Feel free to text me," Bill said, with a small tip of his head toward Ted.

Not wanting to appear to Ted as though I didn't trust him, I laughed and turned away from Bill as he walked to his car.

"I'm not trying to make you uncomfortable," Ted said.

"Oh, no, you're not," I told him. "It's just ... a thing. My boss looks out for me."

"Smart." He looked around the lot, at the cars driving by, pulling in and out. "I was hoping we could talk a minute," he said.

Talk? About what? "Uh...."

"But that's okay. I know you probably want to get home after a long day at work. It's not important."

It was odd. I mean, the guy was a complete stranger, yet I felt totally at ease with him. I didn't sense any kind of attraction or threat toward me, just mild curiosity and ... well, it was weird, but it felt like I was talking with my brother. If I had one. Plus, he had come down here, in front of witnesses, to speak with me.

"Did Marcus tell you to watch me?" I asked.

"Not in those words."

I paused, nodding as I thought. "Hey, do you want to come home with me?"

His eyebrow shot up. "Excuse me?"

"To Marcus' house, I mean. I guess he told you I'm staying there for now." Ted nodded. It was so unlike me to talk to a guy like this. I shook my head, embarrassed. "I know I don't know you, and I'm not trying to pick you up—"

"I know."

"I just mean I'm going to make something to eat and if you haven't had dinner yet.... You said you want to talk, we can do that and eat." Truthfully, being alone in the house didn't thrill me. It was gorgeous, but huge and kind of sterile. Lonely.

"Sounds good," he agreed.

AT THE HOUSE, TED TOOK off his coat, revealing a body almost as muscular and fit as Marcus', though with a little belly where Marcus was flat and hard. He tossed the coat over the back of a chair, as any friend familiar with the surroundings would do. Yet he didn't look comfortable as he stood in the center of the room.

"It's warm in here," he said.

"Mm hm."

"Nice, on a cold day."

I nodded, supposing he was a little uncomfortable with me and talk of the weather might help ease us into a conversation.

"Yeah ... it's really warm in here," he said.

I thought it was perfect, but Marcus was hot every time I touched him—or he touched me—maybe Ted was the same way. "If it's too warm, we could turn the heat down. I don't know how—"

"Hey would you mind if I took my hat off?" he asked suddenly.

"No, of course not. Why would I?"

He shrugged. "Some of us didn't come back looking as pretty as Marcus."

Oh. He was trying to warn me. I felt awful. I gave him a light chuckle, just to let him know I wasn't worried about whatever he had concealed under that cap. "Please, take your hat off."

He pulled it off, and I held a gasp in check. Not that he looked gruesome—not really that bad—but it was unexpected. Most of his right ear was gone, and the extent of the burns was visible now, as was the suture scar across his temple.

When he turned to toss his hat on the couch, he revealed the final path of the scar, up behind his ear, through a patch of skin where hair struggled to grow. To think any human would have gone through that.... I almost shuddered but couldn't risk him thinking it was because of his appearance.

"I was better looking than Marcus at one time. Believe that?" he asked.

"I do," I said. "You're pretty hot now." I laughed. I was only trying to make him less self-conscious. I hoped he didn't think I was coming on to him.

He tipped his head. "I can't wait to tell him that."

I didn't see Tilda when I came in, which meant she was sleeping in the kitchen where Marcus had set her up with a comforter this morning before he left.

"I promised you food...." I said, starting toward the kitchen. Ted followed. "My dog is here somewhere."

"Oh?"

He sounded surprised she hadn't heard us come in. "She's deaf," I said.

"Oh."

Tilda was enjoying the sleep of the blissfully ignorant, curled up like a large bagel on the blanket near the stove. I nudged her gently with the toe of my shoe and she woke with a start, got to her feet, yawned, and stretched. When she saw Ted, she trotted over, tail wagging.

"She's a sweet girl, isn't she?" he said, crouching immediately to scratch her head and return her nuzzles. "What a pretty girl, yes you are."

It made me happy to see someone appreciate Tilda for the loving dog she was. I knew right then I was right to bring Ted here. It also made me feel better about Marcus. He wasn't as emotionally demonstrative as Ted, perhaps, but to miss his dog, and to have a friend like Ted, said a lot about him.

"I'm not at all sure what's here exactly," I told Ted. "Marcus had boxes delivered from the grocery store and the guy came right in and put everything away."

"He hates the grocery store. Always has it delivered," Ted said, giving Tilda a kiss on her head and standing to go to the fridge. "I gave him some suggestions. Let's see what we have to work with here."

Tilda came to stand by me, strategically placing her head under my palm, as Ted pulled items from the fridge and pantry.

"Should I know what to do with..." I leaned over the counter to read the label on a bottle he held. "...truffle oil?"

"No. *I* know what to do with it. How do you feel about lamb chops and truffle risotto?"

I laughed. "If you know how, sounds great."

"Marcus didn't tell you I'm a chef?" he asked.

I shook my head, but smiled. I liked this guy better every minute. "Where?" Not that it mattered. If he was a high-end chef, I wouldn't know any fancy place he mentioned.

"*Bella Segreto.*"

Yup, I was right. I pursed my lips and nodded, impressed never-the-less. He smiled and went back to work.

"What did you want to talk about?" I asked when he was underway with preparations. I'd been wondering since the minute he mentioned it.

"I guess I want to know what your intentions are," he said, not looking up from chopping mushrooms.

I waited for him to laugh. He didn't. "My intentions? For my life? Or for Marcus in particular?"

"Both," he said, using the knife to accentuate.

"Uh...." What was I supposed to say to that? "I plan to look into nursing school as soon as I can afford it. And I'm going to talk to my friend when she gets home from work to ask if I can stay with her for a while, though I don't know what I'm going to do with Tilda...." I looked down at her laying at Ted's feet, hoping some morsel would fall. "Her landlord doesn't allow pets." I swallowed the sudden lump in my throat.

Ted looked at me. "And Marcus?"

I lifted a hand and let it fall. "I have no intentions where he's concerned. He was a ... surprise. I'm not trying to marry him, if that's what you're asking. I just met him. We haven't even dated or anything." Ted looked at me strangely. "I mean, he picked me up once, and we went for a short drive.... That's it." I turned my head to consider him more thoroughly. "In fact, you probably know more about what's going on than I do. You're his friend."

"Well, he surprised me when he spoke about you last night."

"What did he say?" I asked.

"Not a lot. He's never spoken to me about a woman the whole time I know him. Not even what's her name that he broke up with. And I found it odder still, that he would go to the trouble to come over and then not say much of anything."

"Well, he had to say *something*."

"He told me this girl," he gestured to me, "needed a place to stay and it would be cool if I stopped by to see how she's doing."

"That's it?"

"No. He told me you work at All You Can Brew and have blue hair and might be a little skittish."

"He said that?" Skittish? Really? "Why would I be skittish? I'm fine with people. Just fine. It's only him that makes me nervous." I felt myself getting wound up, temper flaring, and took a breath. "I'm not skittish."

Ted smirked.

"He didn't tell you ... anything?" Like what happened at my house. Ted shook his head. Maybe Marcus didn't want him to know for whatever reason, so I wouldn't say anything either.

"I couldn't believe he would take you in," Ted said. "He's a very private person and doesn't invite people into his inner sanctum," he finished, waving the knife around.

Pity. Like taking in a stray dog. I glanced down at Tilda. "I guess he felt stuck with me under the...." I didn't want to say *circumstances* and risk having Ted ask what they were.

He paused his efforts. "How did you meet?"

"He's been coming into the coffee shop for a few months. Then one day, about a week ago, he finally spoke to me."

"Wait, he's been coming for months and only talked to you recently?" he asked.

I nodded, getting the impression that was out of character for Marcus.

"He might not have spoken to me at all if he didn't think I was being bullied."

"Were you?" Ted's spine straightened, and I recognized that same protectiveness Marcus possessed.

"No.... Well, in his opinion. I was only trying to be nice."

Ted shook his head, dismissing my excuse. "You have to understand, Marcus and me, we're protectors. We'll step in anywhere, in any circumstance, and sometimes we're not too smart about it."

Yes, I'd witnessed that firsthand. "It was nothing serious. I let someone talk me into something I didn't want to do and missed my camping trip. It made him angry seeing my weakness, I guess. But I am *not* skittish." The nerve.

"Maybe. He's not good with weakness. Even his own. Especially his own."

He gave me a strange glance and chuckled, but I didn't get the joke.

"He doesn't mean any harm, but I know him long enough to know he can come off like a horse's ass."

I had to laugh then. "I like you."

"Back atcha."

We put all talk of Marcus aside and I did what I could to help Ted with dinner, not that he needed any. The meal was utterly fantastic from the first bite to the last, but he grew tired of hearing me go on about it. The last time I'd had a meal that pleasant was ... never. Not just the food itself, but the company.

Ted was fascinating. Born and raised in Hong Kong to a German father and Serbian mother, he spoke five languages, had won a silver medal in track in the Olympics before joining the service, and had never had a glass of wine in his life.

"Not a sip?" I asked. "Even though you're so into food?"

"Just to see what flavors I'm adding to a dish. It's only a tool," he said. "For me, it would be no different from sitting down with a glass of soy sauce or olive oil. When I drink, it's to get drunk, and there's nothing better at that than whiskey."

After dinner, we cleaned up and chatted about different things, avoiding the military and his injuries, which I had an easier time ignoring than I thought I would. By nine-thirty, he was heading out the door and I couldn't help hugging him.

"Thanks for a pleasant night. I had fun."

"So did I," he said, sounding a little shocked. "Hey, are you sure you don't need anything?"

"No, not a thing," I said, and it was true. I had a full belly, a warm place for me and Tilda, and peace of mind. And, besides stocking the kitchen before he left—including food for Tilda—Marcus had left a small stack of cash with a note, *just in case*, that was now sitting on his dresser awaiting his return.

I watched Ted drive off, then locked up like Marcus had shown me. Hmm. Thinking of Marcus' dresser.... I got Tilda's attention and showed her the way upstairs. I might just take him up on his offer to stay in his room. It really was a great space and when I'd given the bed a light bounce, it felt perfect. I wouldn't mind waking up to a view of the hills.

CHAPTER 9

I WAS GLAD TO BE HOME. I'd spent six and a half long days with a mob of idiot revelers intent on finding pleasure at all cost, which, apparently, ran to almost every girl on the compound rubbing herself against me, promising me things I'd only seen in videos. Well, I hated to tell them I'd done more than I'd ever seen in videos, and wasn't proud of it. In fact, when I thought about it, it made me sick. As did nasty, aggressive women.

I couldn't imagine Serena ever coming onto me that way, and I'd imagined her in more scenarios than I could count. After all, I had plenty of time to fantasize about her, since I hadn't thought of any other woman in a sexual way since meeting her.

No, that wasn't true. It was *before* I'd met her, when I'd only been spying her out behind the coffee shop counter. It was disturbing.

I decided it was time to take things further with her and see if there was really something happening between us, or if I was losing my mind. Teasing her had become teasing me, and these games needed to stop.

My house was empty when I came in. Except for Tilda. Nice dog. Happy and gentle, with sweet brown eyes.

"Hey, Tilda," I said, remembering after that she couldn't hear me.

I rubbed her cheeks and scratched her butt and she followed me to the kitchen, where I got a bottle of water from the fridge and looked down into those hopeful eyes. Her bowl was empty, but I didn't know if that meant she'd already eaten or Serena hadn't fed her yet. Just to be on the safe side, I searched for something to give her.

There were three food containers in the fridge. My containers, not from takeout. I took out the one on top and pulled the lid off. Ted's Chicken Granada. I'd eaten it often enough to know the look and aroma. He told me he was over that first night and had had dinner with Serena. Naturally, there would be left-overs. She ate like a bird.

It might be a little too spicy for the dog, so I put it back and opened the next one. Beef this time, with fennel and green beans. Another of Ted's creations. I gave Tilda a piece of meat, which she snatched without preamble, then sat swishing her long tail across the spotless floor, awaiting more. I checked the last container. Risotto. Ted's. Three meals in my containers meant he'd been here three times, not once.

I don't know what came over me.

Jealousy.

Surprising, but yeah, that was it. I recognized it from my teen years when everything concerning a girl was a big deal, even when it wasn't. It was larger now as it rose in me and stood tall, right beside *Suspicion.*

Why wouldn't Ted mention that he'd dropped by *three* days? That I knew of. Maybe he'd been with Serena the whole time. Maybe they'd gone out the other nights and hadn't cooked here. Or she could have gone to his place.

I tossed Tilda the rest of the meat and was going to dump the risotto in her bowl before remembering her sensitive stomach. I snapped the lid back on and threw the whole thing into the trash.

I did not like this feeling at all. It was crazy. Ted was a friend. The best friend I'd ever had. He'd watched out for me during our time in service and beyond. I'd saved his ass in combat, saw he got home. He'd done the same for me. Ted wouldn't do anything with Serena. He wouldn't betray me.

Right on the heels of this assurance was the awareness that I hadn't told Ted how I felt. I didn't even know how I felt about her, so hadn't given Ted any reason to stay away from her, to not get involved. If anything was happening there, it was my fault. And he didn't have to feel obligated to tell me he'd been having dinner—or anything else—with her.

I turned at the sound of a car pulling up the driveway. My heart began beating faster. Serena.

She walked through the front door, and I swear, it was like my heart fell to its knees. Was she this beautiful when I'd left, or could it simply be the contrast of her inner light with the darkness inhabiting the women I'd been around this last week? Not to mention the darkness inside me right now.

Her eyes lit up when she saw me, and she fired off one of those disarming smiles that made me want to wrap my arms around her and twirl her in circles like in a sappy commercial. Crap. I was in trouble.

"Welcome home!" she said, after locking the door behind her and walking toward me, swinging a plastic bag from her fingers. "I didn't see your car."

I couldn't seem to form a word past the clog in my chest, so lifted my hand in a brief wave. I glanced down at Tilda, who hadn't yet noticed her master, and turned her head toward Serena.

"Look, Mommy's home."

There was something about that phrase coming from my mouth that shook me to the core, and I took a giant step back to distance myself from it. Tilda trotted to Serena, who got down on the floor beside her and nuzzled her furry face. But she was looking at me.

"I guess you left it at the airport?" Serena asked.

"Oh, the car, yeah. Came into New York instead of...."

"For some reason, I thought you were coming back tomorrow."

Maybe I wasn't in trouble. Maybe I was feeling this way because I'd been away. Or because of my survival instinct. Jealousy was a powerful motivator that triggered an instinctive need to defend, to compete. To win. Yeah, that was all this was.

Tilda caught the scent of the bag and pushed her nose into it, but Serena wrestled her head away and stood up, taking the bag with her.

"Are you okay?" she asked me.

"Sure."

"Well, how was your trip?"

"Couldn't wait to get home."

"Are you hungry?" she asked, holding the bag aloft. "Leftovers."

"Let me guess. Ted."

"Yup. Tortellini."

"No, I'm good." So, she'd been with Ted again. My stomach knotted, and it wasn't from hunger.

The closer she came, the more space I found I needed, and being in the same room wasn't doing it. I walked back to the front foyer, swung my duffel over my shoulder, and headed up the stairs.

"Oh!" she called out and ran after me, Tilda chasing after, joining some perceived game.

"What?" I asked, as they passed me on the stairs.

Serena stopped at the landing. "Don't go in your room yet."

"Why?"

"Because it's a mess."

Why would my room be a mess? I kept walking.

"I took you up on your offer to sleep in your room. You're right about the view," she said.

She hurried ahead of me, her antsy behavior and nervous giggle sparking my suspicion even as that annoying spear of jealousy stabbed me under the ribs. What was she hiding? I quickened my steps, marching through the doorway just as Serena pulled up the sheet.

"Sorry," she said, hurrying to the other side of the bed. "I always make the bed, but I was running late this morning."

She was too nervous over an unmade bed. Why? Was she trying to cover evidence she and Ted had been together? In my bed? She hadn't expected me back until tomorrow.

I dropped my bag and ripped the sheet back. I don't know what I expected, but there was nothing there. She looked at me strangely, clutching her hands at her waist.

"What's going on? Why didn't you want me to come in here?"

"I...."

"Serena?"

She looked at the floor, then back at me, her blue eyes guilty. "I let Tilda sleep on the bed with me." She scraped her teeth over her bottom lip. "I didn't want you to find any hair. She sheds—not much. I was going to wash the bedding before you came home, but ... here you are."

My relief was so complete that I actually let out a long sigh. Then I shook my head. Thirty percent to deny Tilda being in my bed was a problem, seventy percent to rid myself of the images of Serena's warm, firm body shifting and rubbing against my sheets.

"I know I shouldn't have let her up on the bed." As if on cue, Tilda jumped onto the comforter. "Tilda, get down." Serena pointed to the floor, but the dog turned in a circle and settled in. She tried to tug the animal by the collar, but Tilda let out a snort and fell over on her side. "Tilda."

"She's okay, leave her," I said.

Serena smiled. "She's not used to nice things and once she got on your bed, now she thinks she's a princess." She chuckled, then paused, her smile gradually fading. "Marcus.... What did you think was going on in your bed?"

"Nothing."

The smile vanished. All of it, replaced by a scowl, her eyebrows arrowing downward. "You thought ... that I had been in here with someone?"

I couldn't answer. Now that she said it aloud, it sounded completely ridiculous.

"With who? Like I'd bring a stranger to your home?" Her eyebrows moved to the next phase of disbelief, arching high over eyes shimmering with temper. "Not a *stranger*. Ted."

"Seren—"

"Ted? *Your friend* Ted?"

She rolled those glorious eyes and spun in a circle. "You're amazing. Truly amazing."

"I'm not accusing you," I said, taking a step closer.

She didn't move, but narrowed those eyes. "Sounds like you are. And Ted! The guy thinks of you like a brother. More. You're like his ... hero or something. What's wrong with you?"

I felt more foolish the longer she spoke, and rightfully so. When I told Ted about this—and I would—I wouldn't be surprised if he punched me right in the face. I deserved it.

"He talks about you so much, with such ... awe, I would have thought you two were gay, if I didn't know for a fact that neither of you are."

Foolish gave a little ground to *suspicion* once again. Ted wasn't gay, but why was she *so* certain? "You find him attractive, don't you?"

This time, disbelief took the form of a pinched face and an incoherent sputter as she lifted her palms up, then let them drop to her sides.

"What on earth does that have to do with anything? He's your friend. He would never hurt you."

"Would you?"

The words were out before I could stop them. Now that they were, they hung there in the space between us, echoing the revelation. *Would you?* meant that she *could*. And that was too troubling to consider right now. I just hoped she didn't grasp the significance.

WHAT EXACTLY DID HE MEAN by that? How could I hurt him? "I wouldn't hurt you, Marcus, even if it was possible."

His brows dipped between his dark eyes. "What does that mean?"

I shrugged, looking away, but he reached out and took me by the arm, causing gooseflesh to erupt over my skin and bringing my gaze to his intense face.

"It means if I'm dating someone, I'm with that person, that's it. I wouldn't cheat on him."

"No, I meant the part about it not being possible to hurt me. You don't think I have feelings?"

"Of course you have feelings," I said. "I meant not toward *me*, that's all."

Something deep inside, and creeping nearer the surface, wanted to refute my own words. There had been fleeting moments when I questioned whether he felt more than the blatant lust he projected. Sure, it could be my own twisted perception, my heart wanting to believe he cared, because my feelings for him were growing every day, even when he wasn't here, but I couldn't ignore the fact that he seemed almost jealous of me and Ted. Didn't that mean he cared at least a little?

Though, that had the ring of an abusive relationship in the making, didn't it?

Unless it was simply a *guy thing*. I knew men had different *codes*. Some wouldn't let a friend sleep with anyone they had slept with. Some didn't want friends even buzzing around any girl who'd so much as blipped once on their radar. I couldn't pretend to understand it.

I gently removed my arm from his grasp. "I'm not interested in Ted that way. But let's not forget, you and I aren't dating, so the point is ... pointless."

He glared at me, like he wanted to whip back a smart-ass reply, but came up empty. What could he say? I was right.

"I want to talk to you about that," he said, at last.

"About what?"

I gave Tilda a little poke and gestured for her to come with me as I started for the doorway. She followed with reluctant steps. Right now, I wanted to get out of that room, away from his presence.

My word, had he been this good-looking the last time I'd seen him? His face, shadowed with stubble, his T-shirt clinging to a body that appeared sculpted from granite.... And for the first time, I saw the tattoo on his arm. Something with wings. I looked back at Tilda, more to keep my gaze off him than to see what she was doing.

"I thought we could have dinner tomorrow," he said, following at my heels along with Tilda.

I froze. "Why?"

He bumped into me. Tilda kept going out the door.

"What do you mean, why? I think it'll be a change of pace from you eating in every night," he said.

There was a definite tone. Displeasure?

"I didn't eat in tonight."

"Yeah, I know, you went to Ted's."

"And that bothers you?"

"Eat anywhere you want," he fired back, annoyed.

"Well, usually Ted comes by here. And he's a fantastic chef."

"Yes. Isn't he?"

Yup, there it was again, that annoyed tone. A muscle in his jaw tightened and released.

"Is something wrong?" I asked. "Did I do something I should know about?"

Marcus looked down at me, his gaze flicking from my eyes to my lips and back. "No. Nothing."

I remembered then, with striking clarity, the times we'd kissed. The searing sensuality I'd experienced with him. That energy and heat seemed concentrated and restrained in the man before me, vibrating to cut loose.

Of course, I may have been wrong. That need could be coming from me. His proximity was cutting off my air supply and increasing the temperature in the room. Just when I thought he would lean over and kiss me, he lifted a hand and stroked my cheek with his thumb.

"You've done nothing at all," he said. "It's me. It's all me." He tilted his head. "Well, not *all* me. I know something's going on—"

I shook my head. "Ted and I are—"

"Not with Ted. With us."

I couldn't deny it. It was there, right in front of me, like a fiery tower, standing over me, daring me to touch it and get burned. Whatever this was, it was hot, and it was dangerous, and I wanted to get closer. What was wrong with me? And why was my heart suddenly pounding in my throat?

"And it occurs to me I don't know you that well," he said. "I'd like to change that. I mean, we are living together."

He touched my cheek again, and I felt the heat of his thumb across every millimeter. My throat was dry, my blood roaring in my ears. I broke eye contact in an act of self-preservation.

"I ... I can't do dinner tomorrow," I said, looking away. "I'm closing at the store. I'm there until eleven."

"Okay, what about...." He closed his eyes. "You don't work on Friday."

"I'm covering for Joy."

"Again?" There was no missing the irritation in his voice.

"Yes. I had nothing to do, and she has a party—"

"You don't...." He raised a hand. "You don't have to explain to me, Serena."

He turned to go, but I touched a hand to his hard abs and he froze. "What do you want me to say? Joy asked. I said yes."

"I just told you not to explain to me."

"I feel like I have to."

"Well, you don't," he snapped.

HER TRYING TO ACCOMMODATE everyone else made me angry enough. Now she was trying to accommodate me. This was exactly what I wanted her to stop. And the repentant look on her face....

"I want you to stand up for yourself, that's all. I can't make you. But when will you tire of people who don't think twice about you, walking all over you?"

"I don't see it that way. Not always." She shook her head. "And when I let them, it's always something stupid. I wouldn't let anyone push me around or anything."

"No?"

She was nervous. An aspect of her personality that bullies zeroed in on. I knew the mentality. I was trained to see weakness in others and to use it to my advantage. I couldn't have her allowing that any more. Was it bullying to determine for her what behavior she should stop? Maybe. But it was for her own good.

"Can you tell her you changed your mind?"

She looked horrified at the suggestion. "No. I won't."

"Why not?"

"Because I told her I would. I made a commitment."

"What about committing yourself to doing what *you* want and not bending every time she asks?"

"And how do you know what *I* want when you're so busy trying to get me to do what *you* want?"

I opened my mouth to deny it—though I don't know why. She was right—but she spoke over me.

"You know, it's really none of your business. I'm not some waif who showed up on your doorstep looking for a step dad—"

"Step dad?"

"—and someone to take care of me. You offered to let me stay here, no strings, as I recall."

"Yes, I did—"

"You never mentioned following rules or running my schedule by you for approval."

"I'm not—"

"And I plan to get out as soon as I can," she said. "When my friend's roommate leaves, I can probably move in with her."

"Serena, I'm not—"

"If that's not soon enough, I can—"

"Serena."

My tone was sharp enough to get her attention if not frighten her a little, but it had to be done. She swallowed, and I paused for a breath.

"I'm not looking for you to go," I said. "If you want to let her use you—" Serena rolled her eyes at me, "—that's on you. I won't bother you about it."

Satisfied, she folded her arms and gave me a confirming nod, her dual-color hair swinging forward and back.

We stood in silence for a moment; her looking like she was waiting for me to say something, me suddenly dealing with a wave of something I'd never faced before. Uncertainty. I still wanted to get to know her better, still wanted to take her out, where we could talk on neutral ground, and I didn't know if she would accept if I asked again. On top of it, I didn't know how I would respond if she declined. And what if....

Wow, was this what insecurity felt like? I dragged a hand through my hair and turned in a circle.

"Are you okay?" she asked.

"I...." I didn't know. Was I?

My old training kicked in. *Fake it till you make it.* When surrounded by enemy personnel, you'd better make them think you were only seconds away from rescue, that they'd be lucky to survive the next few minutes. Confidence had saved my ass more than once.

"Yeah, I'd still like to take you out. If tomorrow's not good, what about Saturday?"

Her shoulders relaxed, her mouth softening into a calming smile. She really was pretty, with a fresh, wholesome look. Like her image belonged on a bar of soap. A clean, pure white bar.... Skimming down warm, wet, slippery skin.... My body tightened everywhere.

"Saturday's fine. I get off at six," she said.

I forced the knots in my stomach to unravel and straightened my spine. "Meet you at the front door around seven-thirty?"

She giggled and my chest did this not so pleasant, but somehow expected, quivering thing, like a laugh was about to rumble out, but decided at the last second to keep the joke private.

"Perfect," she said.

We circled one another slowly, then branched off in separate directions, her to see to Tilda, me to make a phone call and ponder my life choices.

CHAPTER 10

I CHECKED MY WATCH and glanced up the stairs. Seven twenty-seven. Punctuality was important, but never had I waited like this for a woman. Anticipating. Eager. Off balance. A moment later, a door closed upstairs and Serena appeared at the top of the staircase.

"I'm here, I'm here, don't leave without me," she joked, pulling on her black jacket and hurrying down in black, knee-hi boots with spiky heels and a zipper.

Following the boot to the top, my gaze hit knee, then thigh, about six-inches of it until a black skirt swirling around her legs as she moved obstructed my view of flesh. Tucked into it was a glittery pink blouse with an open collar. I didn't know how she could look simultaneously hot and sweet, but she pulled it off exceptionally well.

"Wow." I hadn't meant for the word to spill out, but it made her hesitate and send me a smile that hit me dead center in my chest. Of course, I had to play it off as run-of-the-mill male appreciation, and gave her a wink. "You clean up nice."

Serena giggled, further tightening my chest, and I forced my gaze from her body to her head. She wore her hair up, somehow masterfully tucking away all that blue so that not the barest hint showed. I felt like I knew a secret about her no one else would know tonight, and I found that simple knowledge almost as arousing as the long curve of her neck. I had the strongest urge to kiss her there, right where her throat met her jawline.

"Is something wrong?" she asked.

"No."

But she kept her eyes on me until her smile faded. "You don't think this is too much, do you?" she asked, looking down at herself. "I don't know where we're going, so—"

"You're perfect."

Serena smiled hesitantly. "So are you. Great suit."

It was one of my favorites. I brushed a hand down the front of the blue Armani jacket and stepped toward the door.

"I hope you like Indian," I said, once settled in the car and out on the main road.

"I haven't had it often, but I really liked what I had," she said.

Silence filled the cabin for several minutes and I couldn't help wondering if she was thinking of other times I'd had her alone in my car. I know I was.

The first time, she'd been a ball of nerves, afraid of what I might do to her. I had wanted her edgy then, but not now, and thankfully, she didn't seem nearly as bad tonight. Maybe the nerves were gone, since we more or less shared a house and knew one another a little better. Or maybe they were skillfully suppressed beneath the surface.

Then again, she might be thinking of the next time, when I'd virtually seduced her in front of her coworkers. It wouldn't help my current predicament to think of that, so I made some inane comments about the climate being unseasonably cold for this time of year—which it wasn't, but she agreed anyway.

Next, we tackled the subject of traffic signals and why they always seemed to be red when we were in a hurry, and green when we wanted to sip our coffee.

After a brief pause, she looked at me and asked what I'd done in the military before going into private security. The directness of the question told me it was something that had been bobbing around in her mind for a while, but I wasn't about to discuss my career or past incursions, so I deflected by looking at my dash instruments and announcing we needed gas. If she noticed the gauge read full, she didn't mention it.

Thankfully, she ran into the mini convenience store, and by the time she came out with a pack of peppermint gum, had forgotten the question and didn't seem to notice the car had finished filling in less two minutes.

At the restaurant, I had the host seat us at a table in the back. I picked this place because of its secluded booths, staff that didn't hover, and clientele that were generally reserved, so we wouldn't have to raise our voices and risk being overheard. There was no telling where the conversation could go, and while I wasn't an avid conversationalist when it came to myself, I had every intention of getting Serena talking. I wanted to know everything about her.

I helped her navigate the menu, and we ordered, but nothing too spicy or pungent. There was almost no chance this night would pass without me kissing her, and I didn't want to have to think about my breath.

She folded her hands in her lap and leaned toward me across the table. "So, you won't tell me what you did before private security?"

I laughed. What can I say? It was right there and fell out. "Now, why do you want to know that?"

"Because you seem set on *not* talking about it. I have a natural curiosity."

Yes, I knew all about her natural curiosity as well as I knew my inclination to exploit that curiosity.

"It's just that I've noticed one thing the military men I've met have in common is they love talking about their time in service." She shook her head. "Well, not Ted, he's like you."

"Some things are better left buried."

"I didn't mean to upset—I was just curious."

It wasn't a sharp rebuke, but she looked like I'd slapped her and I reached over the table to cover her hand with mine. There was more happening here than she was letting on.

"You're not that curious about the glories of war and death. What are you hiding?"

She blinked. "What do you mean?"

"You're trying to divert my attention from you."

Her face went blank, like she couldn't figure out how I'd read her mind. "No, I'm not."

I leaned halfway across the table. "Never lie to me."

DINNER WAS A LITTLE TENSE at first, with Serena searching my face several times, like she wasn't sure if I was angry. I hadn't meant to sound harsh, only to express my frustration at having my questions blocked before I could ask them. Yes, I had bitten off a word or two, but only in my haste to relinquish my turn to speak, so I could hear her again. I loved her mild voice, the gentle rise and fall, patterned after a breeze on a summer day, if I had to guess.

If I was given to poetic thoughts.

Which I wasn't.

And the way she was looking at me.... I didn't know if I'd ever seen that look in a woman's eyes. Not even Heidi's, and she'd claimed to love me right up to the day she walked out. But Serena....

Forgiving girl that she was, she soon started opening up, though not about her family. Having met her mother, that was understandable, and I decided I didn't need to know *everything* this first night. Instead, I contented myself with stories of her relationships with childhood friends, most of them involving her best friend, Lisa.

"I mean, can you imagine the shock of a black girl from the streets of Newark moving to a suburb like Chatham?" Serena asked. "She said it was like stepping into a negative."

We laughed, which led to a brief discussion and our agreement that we really were all the same race. Didn't anyone research anymore?

"Knowing you, Lisa didn't feel out of place too long," I said, finally.

"No, she didn't. And she would have told me, believe me. We've always been absolutely honest about everything, right from the start."

"So, you grew up in Chatham?"

I thought I could slip the question by without causing her to clam up, and I was right, at least partially.

"No," she said. "My grandmother lived there, so I stayed with her when my mother ... couldn't take care of me. And we used her address so I could go to school there."

Then, like a flip of a switch, she changed the subject to favorite meals her grandmother would make, which somehow got me reminiscing about my first trip to a drive-thru, on my own, not with my parents.

Though for all her smiling and carefree banter, I sensed the tension underneath and couldn't help wondering if its cause was the same as mine.

It might not be about hiding herself from me, but from trying to evade this magnetic draw, this powerful ebb and flow of energy between us that was both pleasant and maddening and had my nerves stretched about as tight as they could go.

When the meal was over, she opted out of dessert, which was just as well. The sooner we got home, the sooner we could go our separate ways, her to her room, me to mine, dooming myself to a long, restless night, imagining her in my bed.

Tilda was asleep in the kitchen when we got home, happy as ever to see Serena, and me, too. I fed the dog while Serena went upstairs, then I put on a pot of coffee. If I was going to be awake thinking of her, I might as well be really awake and review some files, or get some paperwork done.

As the dog crunched away on her kibble, one or two escaping and rolling away in her hurry to swallow them down, I patiently waited for the coffee to dribble into the pot below. I heard Serena's voice upstairs and at first thought she was talking to me, but then I heard the word *joy*.

My attention immediately and entirely zeroed in on the one-sided conversation funneling down the steps. I came out of the kitchen in time to catch Serena's eye and watch her pivot in the middle of the staircase and head back up, phone pressed to her ear as she tried to keep her voice lowered.

"Uh, that's not ... I don't think I can. Can I call you back?" Serena asked the caller.

I knew what it was before I caught up to her at the top of the landing, ending the call and wrapping both hands around the phone as though trying to conceal the evidence that Joy had manipulated her once again.

"Let me guess," I said. "Joy."

Serena rolled her eyes and let out a little sigh.

"What now?" I asked, unable to mask my exasperation. "Is she donating bone marrow and needs you to fill in? Working at a soup kitchen?"

"I ... nothing," Serena said. "It's nothing."

She jogged down the stairs and a few moments later, I heard the jingle of Tilda's leash and collar as they headed out for a walk. Of course, she would try to avoid me, and I should just let her go.

Instead, I waited in the guest room she was now occupying, across the hall from my room. Her initial shock at seeing me sitting on her bed told me she must have assumed I was in my room. She nipped her bottom lip and my gut tightened, pushing me to my feet.

"What's up?" she asked, folding her arms, trying to look nonchalant, though she'd taken a step back.

"I want to talk to you," I said. "About Joy."

"This again?" she asked, swinging her arms out and dropping them to her sides.

"Yeah, this again."

"Seriously, you make me feel like I'm home with my mother."

I have to say, that pulled me up short for an instant. Then it ticked me off.

"I'm not trying to bust your chops." I leaned over her, more to get closer to her than to make my point, but quickly realized my mistake when I captured that intriguing scent she wore tonight. My gut tightened further.

"Then what do you call it?" She shook her head, refolded her arms. "There's no point, anyway. I already told you I won't let anyone push me around."

"No?"

Since we were by the door, I closed it with my foot, Tilda sitting in the hall, me and Serena inside, face to face. I leaned in again until she stumbled back against it.

"Stop me."

CHAPTER 11

"**S**TOP YOU FROM WHAT?" she asked.

"From pushing you around. From exploiting your weakness and taking what I want."

She laughed, a sound full of nerves and uncertainty, and tried to turn to open the door, but I blocked her with my body, keeping my hands at my sides. I wanted to teach her a lesson, not scare her.

She managed to turn, gripping the handle, but found no room to maneuver the door open.

"Marcus, knock it off."

"Make me." I moved closer, my body instantly responding to the tension.

"This is different," she said, but her voice caught a little.

"No, it's the same. People take from you, a little at a time, every day. And it eats away at you, a little at a time, every day. It's as serious as this." Her hair was still swept up, and I lowered my mouth to the tender skin of her neck right below her ear. "Only now you don't think I'll go any further. You think you're safe, that you can rely on my conscience to make me do the right thing."

She swallowed.

"How does that theory work with other people, Serena? Do they realize they're taking advantage and do the right thing?"

She took a long breath through her nose and shook her head, making me feel like a jerk. But I still had a lesson or two for her.

"Make me stop," I told her.

"I get the point you're trying to make, Marcus. You can stop now."

"*Make* me," I repeated.

She gave me a half-hearted shrug and pushed back against me, but I held my ground. She pushed again, a little more aggressive, and I eased back enough so that she could turn around, but captured her hands, holding them loosely to her sides.

"Not good enough. You're going to have to stop it." She twisted, but I held on, though she could have slid free with very little effort.

"Marcus...."

I had no intention of going further and I really didn't want to scare her, but I held her there another moment to illustrate my point. It was a moment too long when I breathed in her scent once again and was swept away.

My goal of teasing her, toying with her, upended, and in a fraction of a second, I realized my asking her to stop me wasn't about asserting herself, but a plea for her to help me do what I might not have the strength to do myself.

The shoe was now on the other foot and I was the one being *handled*. It had never happened to me before, yet I recognized it had been coming since the first time I saw her, and that all my attempts to knock her off balance then were really pre-emptive strikes to push her away before....

Before what? Before she could hurt me? How was that possible unless I cared for her? I did, but ... I hardly knew the girl. Besides, I'd pursued her, not the other way around.

"I want you, Serena. I want this. Make me want to stop more than I want you."

I couldn't believe I'd admitted to her that I wanted her this way. She probably thought I was just horny.

"Please," she said, her voice a thin thread wavering up between us.

I bowed my head, so that I spoke into her ear. "That sounds like a request. Like you want me to keep going."

Even so, I released her hands at once, about to back off, when she brought them to my waist and gripped my shirt. She closed her eyes, scraping her teeth over her bottom lip.

As much as I was trying to teach her, I'd just learned something very important. She didn't want me to stop.

Caught up in the shock of the revelation, I'm still not sure who made the first move, but our lips fused together, separating only long enough to pull shirts over our heads and gasp for air.

Half hopping, half shuffling, the backs of my legs bumped against the bed and I tumbled with her, twisting my body to pull her on top of me so I didn't crush her.

The headboard banged against the wall as we crashed onto the mattress, my arms full of her soft curves, lungs full of her breath, thoughts full of what came next.

My body tingled, burned, like someone had doused me with gasoline and set me on fire. I swear, I'd never undressed myself or a woman so fast.

But I had to ask. I might regret it, but I had to ask... "Are you sure about this, Serena?" I panted.

She kissed me again. Her seeking hands found me, by accident, it seemed, when she jerked her hand away. Should've known then. But her hand brushed my nipple, and I forgot what it was I should have known.

"Marcus."

It was more sigh than murmur. I loved hearing my name escape those beautifully parted lips. I cruised my mouth down to her collarbone, my hands roaming where they pleased. Wow, she was beautiful. She raised her hips toward me, moaning and writhing as I returned to her mouth and began a deep exploration with my tongue even as her smooth fingertips ventured over my skin.

It was a simple matter of tilting my hips to move into position. She gripped my triceps then, and kissed me harder.

I groaned, my breath tangling in hers as we joined and moved together, and I was almost instantly swept into a current of sensation such as I'd never known before.

My mind raced, then ground to a standstill, then tore off again. All the while telling me that as incredible as making love to her was ... something wasn't right.

In fact, something was very, very wrong. But she clutched my shoulders, sighed my name, and I lost the will to consider what it might be.

No, that wasn't true. I knew. I knew, dammit, and in that moment, could do nothing about it.

I CAN'T DENY THAT WAS one of the best experiences of my life, but as I lay there panting, dragging air through my lungs, I dreaded moving, looking down into eyes that must be disturbed or full of something I didn't want to see.

So, I did what any coward would do. I avoided eye contact as I parted from her and slid to the edge of the bed to catch my breath while I hung my head and cursed myself inwardly for the better part of a minute.

She touched my bare skin, and I surged to my feet, unashamed by my nakedness. I'd stolen her first time and she could never redo it. And if that wasn't bad enough, I did the *worst* thing a coward could do.

I blamed her.

"Why didn't you tell me?"

"Marcus—"

"No! How could you do that to me?"

"I—"

I let out a vile expletive—again directed at me—and looked down at her. "Are you kidding me?"

"Mar—"

"What the hell were you thinking? Why didn't you tell me you'd never done it before?"

I was furious. Livid. At myself. The instant I'd realized her *state*, I hadn't been able to change my course. Like a man possessed, determined to find my satisfaction despite the alteration of circumstances. Though, honestly, it was too late at that point. I'd never—and I mean never—put my needs ahead of a woman's in the bedroom.

I dragged in another breath. Hating myself did nothing to calm me, or to lessen my desire when she looked up with trembling lips and sad eyes. Damn, I would take her again if I wasn't careful. The best I could do was keep talking and hope my still aroused body returned to normal quickly.

But looking at her with her hair loose now, twisted in every direction, and her lips swollen from mine, that would not happen. I had to think of something else. The news. That was always grim. A freighter sank yesterday off the coast of … somewhere foreign.

No, that didn't do it. I thought of sinking into her.

There was that update on the man trampled by shoppers while opening the doors of a department store last Christmas. Critical condition. Might not regain full brain activity.

That should have done the trick, but the thought of people flooding inside the door reminded me of my climax and— Crap, what if she got pregnant?

"What if you get pregnant?" I asked her.

A tiny line formed between her brows.

"I mean ... there's a chance ... unless it's not time in your cycle ... or whatever." Talking like that gave me the willies, but we had to discuss it. Idiot that I was, I should have taken the initiative. I had condoms in my room, but I'd been too wound up, like a freaking teenager.

"I won't. I probably won't," she amended with a shake of her head. "I'm on the pill."

I tilted my head. "Why are you on birth control if you're not having sex?" I would bet my life she had been a virgin just minutes ago.

"I get bad cramps. Like ... bad," she said, gesturing with her hands. "The pills help."

That made no sense to me, but I was glad she had protection. Damn, I couldn't believe how uneasy I felt. I paced to the window, then back, looking down at her for what seemed like minutes before sitting beside her on the bed, resting my hand between us and brushing her thigh with my pinky. She moved her leg out of reach.

The silence continued to stretch between us, making an already uncomfortable situation almost unbearable. Finally, I turned toward her, raised my hand palm up, then let it drop to the bed.

"I don't know how to be this," I said. "This ... *afterglow, say the right things, guy.*"

"Obviously," she agreed. "But I'm not asking you to."

She smiled at me then. Not a full one, but enough to irritate me all over again. She deserved better than this, and I couldn't take it back. How did I fix it? Accepting there was no way wasn't an option.

"You're probably sore," I said.

"A little."

"That's to be expected. It'll pass."

I cringed at the sound of my voice. Coarse. Dismissive. How could I have been so careless with her? This was a pivotal event in a girl's life, and I'd taken her like a seasoned.... Next time I would make it better for her. And, oh yes, I'd already decided there would be a next time.

"Something wrong?" she asked.

"No. No." What was I saying? "Yes! I took your virginity, Serena. Do you have any clue what that means? How I'm feeling right now?"

"Uh...."

A tear crested in her right eye and tumbled over the edge to the soft lashes beneath. What the hell was I saying? I'd just stolen the most precious thing she had to give without really giving her a chance to slow things down or talk, and I was blaming her. How was *she* feeling?

I took her hands in mine. "I'm sorry."

When she tossed her head, that lone tear dropped to her cheek and rolled until I kissed it away, licking the warm, salty liquid from my lips. Never before had I kissed a woman's tears away, but this seemed expected, natural. I rested my forehead against hers and squeezed her hands, but she removed them and folded them in her lap.

"Did I hurt you?" I asked, afraid she would be honest and tell me it hurt like hell. I wanted her to spare my feelings, even though I didn't deserve it. The thought of hurting her in any way was more than I could take right now.

"IT WASN'T TOO BAD," I said, struggling to recall if I was actually lying.

No, I wasn't. It hurt like a bubble of pain had burst open in my core, but a minor bubble, not half as bad as I'd heard. I wondered if my feelings for him were even now helping to dull the memory of the pain. I'd heard the same thing happened with childbirth.

Still, I ached, deep inside, and as much as I wanted it to be a wonderful ache that I would remember forever when I looked back in a romantic haze, there was no way to ease it. And was it any wonder? I'd been astounded when I finally dared to look at his.... I had trouble even thinking the word.

Heat climbed my cheeks when my eyes wandered between his legs. I almost let out a nervous giggle, but masked it with a cough. At least I thought I had until he shot me a look. He didn't look amused. At all.

I knotted my fingers together in my lap. The silence that slithered in wasn't making me feel any better. I felt alone. Used. As though any woman could have satisfied his sexual need at that moment. It just happened to be me.

And the worst part was, I didn't want reassurance or excuses. I wanted to do it again. It had been hasty and rough, but now that the initiation was out of the way, I thought we could have a much better time now that we were both prepared.

But when I glanced sideways at him, his head down, I could see he was already regretting it, trying, I was sure, to think of some way to get me out of here and never see me again. Could I blame him? It was probably terrible for him.

He'd been enjoying himself at first, but I'd been completely caught up in my head, exploring the new and awesome sensations and paying him virtually no mind. At least that's how I think it happened.

I bristled inside. I hadn't had sex before tonight because I'd refused to be a man's plaything, letting him serve himself while thinking nothing of me, and here I'd gone and done it. Worse, I'd had sex before marriage, something I'd promised myself and my grandmother I wouldn't do.

"I should shower," I said, pasting a phony smile on my lips and scooting off the edge of the bed.

But he grasped my forearm and stood me in front of him, raking his eyes over me, making me feel exposed and powerless. And a little aroused, it shocked me to admit.

"I'm sorry," he said. "You should've told me you were a virgin. I wouldn't have been that rough."

I raised my chin. "Yeah, it was my fault."

It was a crappy thing to do, casting blame on him for any of it when I'd wanted it as much as him, but I was suddenly feeling vulnerable and a little sulky and wanted to be held in the worst way, but couldn't tell him so. If he cared about me, I wouldn't have to tell him. He would know. Right?

A shadow passed over his features and he stood. "Are you saying I forced you?"

Appalled that he'd think that, I grabbed his forearm. "No! No."

"Or that you didn't have every opportunity before today to tell me you'd never done this?"

Well, the subject hadn't come up in this way, but…. I dropped my hand. "You're right, I did."

And again, when he'd first started kissing me against the door. But I hadn't been able to get the words out. Truthfully, it wasn't his fault, because if I'd been able to form words, even if I'd formed *those* words, I would have told him not to stop. Though he probably would have.

I shook my head. "There's no fault one way or the other," I told him, then shrugged. "Or there's double fault both ways. I wanted it to happen. I don't regret it." I had a question, though. "Did I ever lead you to believe I had...?"

"No. Never. But just because I didn't consider you had, doesn't mean I considered you hadn't. Just...." He scraped a hand over his face. "Why me?"

He sounded panicked. Like I'd selected him for the Hunger Games.

"It's a tremendous responsibility. Why did you pick me?"

"I didn't *pick* you, Marcus. It's not like I pulled your name out of a hat or penciled in my calendar, *tonight I'll lose my virginity to Marcus Armatura.* And I'm certainly not holding you to anything because of it. I mean, we don't have to get married, or even date. Whatever."

I tried a smile to lighten the mood, but he didn't smile back, only looked confused, like he was trying to piece it all together. I walked out, leaving him to it. I would try to do the same.

CHAPTER 12

I HADN'T TALKED TO ANYONE about their first time, even Lisa, so I didn't know what I was supposed to be experiencing right now. Bliss? Smug satisfaction? Excitement that I'd crossed some kind of threshold in my life? I was pretty sure the usual healthy response wasn't annoyance with a hint of sadness.

If I'd walked through this moment in fantasies as most girls did, I would have painted the event in gentle pastel strokes. Pinks, greens and yellows maybe. But placid, muted tones didn't fit this event at all. My first time was broadly slashed with moody blues and fiery oranges, splashed with angry reds.

One might say as first times went, mine was a disaster. But that isn't true. It was only the *after* that sucked. Yes, there was a little pain during, but that was to be expected, and what led up to it was ... wow. Never before had my body experienced such an absolute explosion of sensations, washed in a cacophony of emotions, and to the very end, I was precisely where I wanted to be.

Even now I could feel the pressure of Marcus' body on top of mine, the scrape of his whiskered jaw against my cheek, the slide of his tongue over mine, the grip of his fingers entwined with mine, the pressure of him inside me. That sharp, then throbbing pain, that even still was a dull ache, calling back some of those initial sensations. And the heat.

But recalling the *after* dispelled those sensations like a plunge into an icy pond. I couldn't delete the *after* and catalogue my deflowering as a sweet memory. It was all part of the whole, including his reaction, withdrawing from me, and rolling away to puzzle over what *I'd* somehow done to *him*.

I was under the impression a guy would love hearing his was the first flag planted, but then, I had no more experience with the psyche of men than I had with sex. And how had he—the know-it-all, man-of-the-world that he was—had no comprehension that I'd never been there before?

His concern about my getting pregnant would have been sweet at least, if I'd thought it had anything to do with wanting to protect me and not his own concern over fathering a child.

Actually, now that I thought about it as I stepped into the shower, the *before* had been pretty strange, too. He in no way forced me to have sex, it wasn't that. What ticked me off was his persistent insistence that I was somehow weak. Was that what he thought? That I'd given in because I'd been too *nice* to say no?

I mean, did he really want me, or had it been all about trying to make a stupid point and then getting carried away in the moment? That was it, wasn't it? I was an idiot. I'd let him use me as an object lesson. To myself!

If that wasn't it, it left me with only one other reason he'd chosen that time to take me to bed. He was a man of considerable self-control, I'd seen that, so if it wasn't about feelings for me, pure lust, or making a point, then he was trying to *one up* Ted. He'd seemed pretty jealous, so maybe he thought to accomplish the deed and lay claim before Ted could.

The more I thought about it, the angrier I became, until I'd seethed my way through showering, drying, dressing, and brushing out my hair. I heard him banging around downstairs in the kitchen and didn't think I could face being alone with him right now, so called Lisa and told her I was coming over.

"Where are you going?" Marcus asked when I reached the front door.

I thought I'd been pretty stealthy, but he must have been listening for me. "To a friend's."

He stared at me for a good five seconds, looking like he wanted to say something, but in the end gave me a nod and turned to walk back into the kitchen. It was bizarre to watch him, knowing that just an hour ago we'd been in bed, in the most intimate scenario a man and woman can achieve. Me for the first time.

His arms had wrapped around me, possessed me. His shoulders, now covered in the soft cotton of his shirt, had moved under my palms, smooth and hard. His powerful thighs, now concealed by his jeans, had pressed against mine, along with other parts of his anatomy that I could easily bring to my mind's eye.

I felt myself flush and looked away. For all our detailed knowledge of one another's bodies, I seemed to know him less now than I had before.

"I won't be too late," I called out, but he didn't answer. At once I felt like crying and did not know why, so hurried out the door before I broke down.

I kept my tears to myself all the way to Lisa's house. Well, I don't know for sure that I did. By the time Lisa came out to my car to see why I hadn't come in, my face and neck were wet with tears and she said I'd been parked out there for several minutes. She brought me inside, sat me on the couch, and waved off her soon-to-be-former-roommate, Margie, when she asked if everything was all right.

"What the hell happened?" Lisa asked, sitting close to me and taking my hands in her lap.

Her brown eyes held all the compassion I needed, but I didn't want to make her worry, so I started my tale with a nonchalant air. As if I could pull that off. The girl was way too adept at spotting *bs*, especially in me. That, and my eyes were puffy from crying.

My act lasted about ten seconds before Lisa lifted her chin. "Hey," she said. "You're gonna tell me the truth, *exactly* the way it happened."

"Okay."

"I mean it."

I nodded and began my saga again. She already knew about Marcus and our strange meeting, up to the point before my mom's house. No sense dragging him into that story and adding a lot of needless questions. But in order to tell my tale of woe and how I believed he was disappointed in me for bowing to Joy's whims, I backtracked a little to the first time he'd scolded me about her.

"He's right," Lisa said, shaking her head. "I'm always telling you you're too easy going, too easy to take advantage of."

I nodded.

"Am I or am I not always telling you that?" she asked.

"Yes, you are." It was disheartening to know everyone, including my closest ally, saw this dent in my character. Everyone but me.

"Go on," she ordered.

I filled in the gaps she was missing after leaving my mother's house, ending just a couple hours ago with my deflowering.

"I knew it!" she said, raising her hands to the ceiling and letting them fall on my leg with a slap. "I knew you lost it!"

"You did not," I said, laughing.

"I did! The minute I saw you I could tell. You have that ... *look*," she said, waving her hands around my body and head.

I gave her a playful shove. "You are so full of it!"

"Nope." She tapped a finger to her temple. "I know things."

"Right, like your tribal grandmothers," I said, rolling my eyes.

Lisa laughed. "Don't mock the queens, they knew things, and I do too."

"Well, do you know what's next?"

"The only one who knows that is you," she said, in all seriousness.

But I didn't know. "I.... I feel...." What? I didn't know that either. "How did you feel? After?"

Lisa didn't give pat answers. If I asked anything, she would dive into her memories and pull it up.

"I was surprised it was over so fast," she said with a laugh. "Kent was in there one second and out the next. He was freaked out. I mean, I was nervous, but he was ... whew! It was like he was pitching the last ball in a no-hitter for the Yankees and terrified to make a mistake, but wanted it to just be over already." She paused, a ghost of a smile playing on her full lips. "He got better fast, but initially I didn't think I wanted to do it again. It wasn't much fun."

"No, I mean, did you regret doing it at all? Did you feel like you should have waited? Or doubt he was the right guy?"

Lisa shrugged. "I was eighteen, you know that. Every girl wants her first time to be with someone special, but Kent and I had been dating for a couple months straight—longest boyfriend I had to that point. I thought it was serious and ... I guess I wanted to get it over with too. Check it off the to-do list and have one less thing to stress over." She blew out a short breath. "So yeah, I did and didn't regret it."

I thumped my head back against the cushion. "You're not much help."

"Hey, my story isn't yours. You regret it?"

"Yes and no," I said, mimicking her. "I wanted it to happen with Marcus—not that I planned it or anything. But now that it has...."

"Stud's a dud?" she asked with a faux pout.

I giggled. "No, it's ... no," I said, recalling his— I shook my head. "It's not that."

"You don't think he appreciates it as the sacrifice it was?"

I shook my head. "He knows it was a serious moment for me, he gets that."

"It just wasn't for him," Lisa finished.

"No, that's not it either. He was pissed because I didn't tell him beforehand."

Lisa flung herself back on the sofa cushion, eyes wide. "Are you kidding me? Tell me you're kidding!"

"No." Okay, if she was annoyed at me, it must really be a big deal. I mean, I knew it was.... "I thought he knew."

"Serena! Man!"

"What?"

She sat up and stared me directly in the face. "Don't you realize how cheated he must feel?"

Again we were back to him? "Why?"

It was her turn to roll her eyes. "He was your first. Your *first*. That's a huge thing for a guy. Every man wants a virgin. Whether they admit it or not, all men want to be first."

"I know that," I told her.

"But for some, it's not about competition or scoring the big prize. If he's any kind of decent guy—and the fact that you wanted to sleep with him tells me he is, or you wouldn't have—he would have wanted to make it special for you and him. You robbed him of that chance."

She sprung her hands as wide open as her eyes and sat back, letting the reality of her words sink in. I didn't know how it had come to this point. How I'd given my virginity to Marcus and now somehow felt I had to make it up to him. I'd had no pre-conceived dreams of candlelight, soft music and sweet, encouraging words to accompany my first-time. But maybe he would have. If he'd known.

I sighed, long and hard. "Now what?"

"I think you should do it again. This time, let him *make love* to you. The right way," Lisa said.

"That's right!" Margie added, carrying a box from her room and stacking it atop several others by the front door. "And you make love to him right back."

Lisa laughed. "Right."

I wanted to agree, but that last part.... I had no idea how to *make love to him right back*. Was that expected? I figured if we did do it again, I'd let it all happen naturally, but what if Marcus was expecting more? Were there things I was supposed to know instinctively and didn't?

Margie came over and sat on the floor in front of the couch and as she and Lisa talked about preferred sexual positions and the *extras* that made for a fulfilling experience, panic mushroomed inside me. Not so they would notice, but enough to make me think falling back into bed with Marcus might be the most humiliating thing I could do.

He was experienced and maybe used to certain things. What would he want with a girl who laid there like a cardboard cutout while he did all the work? Besides, there was still part of me that wondered if he would even bother. He'd planted his flag, made his point. If that was all there was to it, there was no reason to try to seduce me again.

Try. Yeah, right. I almost laughed out loud. Even with all my doubts and fears, I was liable to dissolve into a puddle of lust if he touched me again.

"Hey." Lisa elbowed me.

"Mm hmm," I said.

She giggled. "*Mm hmm* what?"

"Uh ... whatever you just said. I'm agreeing."

"You have no idea what I said."

"She's thinking about getting some more of that man, that's what it is," Margie said with a wink.

I laughed. Yeah. Yeah, I was. But I couldn't allow myself to let it happen again. For his sake and mine. He was probably as upset and confused as I was and we both needed space and time to adjust. The problem was, how could we get that space and time under the same roof? There would be tension, no question about it. It wasn't fair of me to do that to him.

The answer was under my nose. Well, to my right, stacked by the door.

"So, did you find a roommate yet?" I asked Lisa.

CHAPTER 13

I'D NEVER HAD A VIRGIN. Even when I was one. Wasn't likely to again. As I thought it, standing on the back deck, staring off into the dark woods surrounding my house, I wondered if I would have *any* other woman again. Serena might be it for me. As a man who prided myself on my recon skills, I hadn't paid enough attention. Hadn't seen it coming. She'd crept under my skin and there was nothing I could do.

I shook my head hard, trying to dislodge the four-letter word and wild thoughts that tried to implant themselves. She was a sweet girl, and we'd had sex. That was all there was to it. I was only feeling weird because it had rocked me and I was guilty over the whole thing.

That didn't stop my body from aching for her. Literally. I couldn't wait to get her into bed again. But first we needed to talk. I pissed myself off with the way I'd left things. I hadn't meant to make her think I was angry for not telling me she was a virgin—I mean, I was, initially, but only because I didn't know how to handle it.

It wasn't the surprise of finding her intact. It was my astonishment that she would give herself to me. To *me*. It was a big deal, and I wasn't certain she understood the weight of that on me. Not that I didn't want to bear the responsibility, but it would have been nice to brace for it. To do things differently. To earn it. I should have asked the questions, should have taken it easy with her, should have initiated her with soft caresses and tender kisses.

And here I was thinking of words like *tender* in relation to sex. When had that happened? I threw my head back against the chair, closed my eyes, and groaned into the frosty night air. I had to stop beating myself up over it. There were a few brief moments when I wondered if I'd pushed her into it. Sure, I'd accused her of giving to others what she didn't want to, and granted, my pushing was what got us into the bed, but I knew without question that if she hadn't been totally willing to give herself, it would never have happened.

Anyway, it had happened and was done now, and that was that. Off in the distance, a coyote sent up a mournful wail. Right there with ya, buddy.

The sound of a car coming up the driveway brought me to my feet and the yard light came on as I leaned over the deck rail to see Serena's car come to a stop. My heart was in my throat even before she got out, my stomach in a knot. I resisted the urge to go down the steps and walk her inside. Instead, I went into the house and waited for her to come in the front door.

"Hi," she greeted, lowering her eyes.

"Hello."

She licked her lips, and unless I was mistaken, sucked in a long, shaky breath. She appeared more nervous than me.

"Did you eat?" I asked. I don't know why I asked that. Her eating made me think of Ted feeding her, and that was the last thing I wanted to think about.

She nodded and smiled a little. "Yup. Pizza."

I nodded back, like a dope. A mute dope who just wanted to go to her, kiss her and hold her. It should have been easy, but my feet wouldn't budge.

"Good," I said, finally. "We ate that Indian food ... hours ago." I didn't know why I said that either. If it could have felt any more awkward, I didn't know how.

"You?" she asked.

I shook my head.

She picked at her nails and looked up at me with this heartbreaking sweetness that stole my breath.

"Where's Tilda?" she asked, looking past me toward the kitchen.

"Uh...." Tilda ... Tilda.... "Asleep in the kitchen I think."

Serena smiled and took a step toward me. I knew she meant to go past me to find her dog, but I couldn't let her pass without saying something. Doing something. I stepped in front of her, clasped her by the shoulders and skimmed my hands to her neck, my thumbs sliding over her collarbones.

"Wait," I whispered.

My right thumb grazed her bottom lip, and I lowered my head toward hers.

"No." She shook her head, her small hands wrapped around my wrists.

I released her slowly, reluctantly, but completely, stepping back. "What's wrong?"

"I just...." She lowered her head, then took a breath and met my eyes evenly. "I don't think it's a good idea to get swept away again."

"Probably not." I didn't plan to get swept away this time, but to perform each task mindfully, intentionally.

"We ... did what we did ... but we can't do that again," she said.

I widened my stance and folded my arms out of pure curiosity. Thinking she might read it as intimidating, I uncrossed them.

"What do you mean? Why?" I asked. She swallowed and a tiny line formed between her eyebrows. I did not intend to frighten her. "I'm not saying we should. I'm just asking. Are you all right?"

She nodded, in a hurry to relieve my stress, it seemed. "I'm fine, Marcus. It's ... we don't ... we don't really even know one another. I don't think it was fair to you. I mean, for me not to tell you ... and I'm sorry."

"I—"

"I think we should take a beat and think things over. I'd like to slow things down."

I nodded back. It was probably a good idea. Slow things down. Way down. For her own good and mine. But the word *No* rang inside my head. I knew when a person said they wanted to *slow things down*, it inevitably meant they were pulling away. I'd said it to women often enough.

"Sure. You're right." I heard the words coming from my mouth but couldn't have said where they came from. Or the ones that followed, that sounded wretched and pathetic. "Can we just talk?"

Her expression told me she'd heard it that way, too. Her eyebrows lifted and lowered and she gave me half a shrug.

"Okay, yeah, we should."

She gave me a *hold on* finger, then peeked in on Tilda in the kitchen before walking back into the living room. I followed, because, God help me, I couldn't do anything else.

I sat next to her on the couch, wondering how long I should wait for her to look at me. This entire night so far was surreal, and it was just hitting me that it might be even worse than I'd thought. When her gaze remained fixed on everything but me, I had to speak.

"First, I want to say—"

"I'm moving in with my friend Lisa," she blurted. "Tomorrow."

The best I can describe the feeling of loss was like someone grabbed my internal organs and just ripped them out. It wasn't a devastated feeling like a death, but more that I'd been so close to attaining a particular goal that I hadn't even identified, only to have it snatched away. Was that it? Serena had become a goal for me to conquer, and now I wouldn't have that chance? I wanted to believe that was it.

Hoped that was it.

"Oh."

"I would leave tonight, but her roommate isn't out until tomorrow," she said. "I'm technically not supposed to be there until the first, but under the circumstances...."

I took a breath, lifted my hands, then left them drop. Like it didn't really matter. It was none of my business. But it did, and it was. At least in my head. "I'm in no hurry to be rid of you," I said. "It's not like you're in my way."

"I know, and I appreciate that," Serena said, finally looking at me. "But you've been so nice to me already."

What? Was I hearing this? We had sex a matter of hours ago—her for the first time—and she was saying I'd been *nice*. Had I? Really?

That wasn't the way I remembered it. I remember being short with her, teasing her, testing her, making her feel uncomfortable, and maybe a little scared. But I wanted that chance to be nice to her. And now she was leaving.

"You're going to keep in touch, right?" I asked.

Wow, that sounded cold. Like we hadn't shared an incredibly intimate, life-altering event. Like I couldn't just go over there and see her whenever I wanted.

She nodded. "I can't take Tilda, though," she said. "Lisa's landlord won't allow it."

"Okay." I liked having the old girl around.

"Ted's going to keep her until I find a pet-friendly place."

I felt a boot stomp right in my gut. Size twelve, steel-toe.

"I can keep her here," I said, hoping I didn't sound as needy to her as I did to myself. "I mean, she's already used to the house."

Serena squared her shoulders. "That's all right, Marcus. You've done so much already. Plus, you said yourself you're never here," she added quickly. "She shouldn't be alone so much."

I could tell she wanted to say something else and that I wouldn't like it.

"I ... don't think we should see each other," she finished.

That boot stomped again, and ground in. Even after sex, I'd lost her before I'd even had a chance to fight for her. To Ted, it seemed. Well, maybe that wasn't true. I had had a chance. If I'd been up front from the beginning and admitted my growing feelings for her instead of trying to convince myself I was mainly interested in helping her stand up for herself, I would be holding her right now instead of waiting for her to leave me for another man.

Whoa, wait. I didn't know who this guy was, the one sitting here, agreeing with her, but my voice reached my ears, saying, "Sure, whatever you think's best."

That couldn't be right. I wanted her. I didn't want her to leave. And I wanted her deaf dog to stay right here, too.

I should fight for her. That's what I do. I fight, I convince, I power through a situation and steer it where I want it to go. *Manipulate*, you might call it.

But I don't know what happened. When she rose to go to her room, I found I didn't have it in me to do more than stand with her and shove my hands in my pockets.

Was my weak compliance an attempt to compensate for taking her virginity? A kind of penance? Or did this passive guy, whoever he was, know something I didn't? That I had to let her go, to prove I could.

Whoever he was, he might have the right idea, but for the wrong reason. He probably thought he was falling in love.

Me? I knew a weakness when I saw one.

I couldn't let her become mine.

LISA AND MARGIE HAD almost convinced me to come back here and make love with Marcus all night long. Not that I'd needed that much prodding. I'd teetered a bit, but reason had fully kicked in about halfway back to the house, when I was once again alone with my thoughts and reviewing the evening.

We'd had exactly one date—the same night we'd had sex. Before that, there had been physical attraction and explosive heat, but he'd given me no reason to believe our time together had any romantic or emotional connection. In fact, he'd gone out of his way to make known he was playing some kind of twisted game with me. Pulling my strings, trying to make me do what he thought was right and acceptable.

Okay, he was protective, and I believed he wanted the best for me even though he had a weird, often domineering way of showing it, but protective and romantic were two entirely different things. Holding a gun to Tank's head was protective, not romantic.

In my borrowed room, I sighed aloud and rubbed Tilda's soft head as she slept curled behind me on the mattress. I still found it hard to believe I'd had sex. Sex. With a *man*. Not a groping teenager on prom night, but a fully grown—and oh, was he grown—*man*. It was everything I'd thought and nothing I'd imagined at the same time. But wow, how could I have been so stupid to give myself to a guy who didn't love me?

As far as I knew, he might not even really like me! I was probably more of a *girl improvement* project than anything else. He wanted to tweak me and mold me into his version of a self-reliant female. And for what? Only to let me walk out the door first thing tomorrow?

I'd wanted to believe the look of sorrow on his face when I said I was leaving had been disappointment, but maybe he was simply regretting his poor decisions that brought us to that couch, and that conversation. He had raised no objection, other than an inane comment about not being in a hurry to be rid of me. It seemed like he wanted Tilda more than me.

I mean, when I came back to the house after Lisa's, it was an awkward situation, and he'd tried to kiss me, but what guy wouldn't try to get a girl back in bed for another round? I was wondering if this wasn't all about him feeling abandoned again. First Heidi and Teddy, now me and Tilda.

"Idiot."

I thudded my head against the pillow. But self-deprecation wouldn't help. I needed sleep and didn't know how much I would get after this stressful day and having to relocate tomorrow.

At least I didn't have to work and see Joy's face. Just the thought of her made me angry. Not that any of this was her fault, but ... it kinda was. No more than my own, but she really thought I was an easy mark, didn't she? Well, that had ended. No more covering, no more taking her customers, no more doing her share of cleanup—nope.

Marcus would think I was finally coming to my senses, and maybe I was, but I wasn't doing this to agree with him. I was doing it as a first step in taking responsibility for my happiness.

CHAPTER 14

"THAT DIDN'T TAKE LONG, did it?" Lisa asked, sitting on my makeshift bed and giving it a bounce.

Ted had loaned me the air mattress, along with a pump that blew it up in under a minute. It looked cozy now, topped with a set of Lisa's sheets and one of her pillows. Wish it felt as good. The otherwise empty room had no charm, but it was a cheery yellow, and its one window overlooked the backyard.

The one thing I wished above all else that it did have was Tilda. I dropped her off with Ted and made my escape while she was wandering the house. I felt a clutch in my chest when I imagined her realizing I was gone, looking for, and not finding me. Even now, I had to distract myself from that thought or become a blubbering mess.

I sat beside Lisa, secretly hoping the mattress didn't pop. Could that happen?

She nudged my knee. "This is only temporary, you know. Before long, you'll have an actual bed and things of your own. Start a regular, single girl life."

I glanced down at my bag of belongings, opened at the top and spread to reveal folded clothes and a few books. The smaller things, like my makeup and toothbrush, had fallen to the bottom. They'd had a place for a while in Marcus' house, but like me, had been uprooted.

True, it was my choice to leave, yet somehow that didn't help this hollow feeling that I might never really belong anywhere. Even at home, I hadn't felt wanted. Turned out I wasn't.

I blinked back a sudden sting of tears and turned my face so Lisa couldn't see. She meant well, and I knew she would watch out for me, but I wanted to be alone with my misery for a while. She'd be going off to work soon, and then I was free to sob my eyes out and wander around the empty apartment. Lucky me. At least if Tilda was here, she would offer that quiet assurance that things would work out.

I wanted Tilda. It would be great if I could keep busy and not think about her or when I might be able to reunite with her, but I had nothing but time on my hands. And, hey, if I wanted to see my dog later, I only had to drive to Ted's. Lisa would come, of course. If I was seeing things right, she was interested in him.

When I'd taken her to his house for dinner last week, she didn't stop asking him questions and sending him flirtatious signals, and had called me talking about him hours afterward. And he was every bit as interested in her. Maybe more. He'd jokingly confessed a preference for black women and promised me another free meal for having introduced them.

"I better get going," Lisa said. She patted the bed and stood. "Grab a blanket from my bedroom closet."

"Okay, thanks."

A few minutes later, Lisa closed the front door behind her. I no longer felt like crying, so turned on the TV and flopped onto the couch. Morning shows were the worst, but TV was basically a steady stream of commercials with just enough intermittent pieces of show to keep you hooked until the next barrage of commercials. It was one reason I didn't own a TV.

After my fifth viewing of a commercial for a battery-operated mop, I heard a car door outside and went to the window.

No way. Couldn't be.

But it was.

I took the biggest breath I could manage, then pulled the door open right before my mother's bony knuckles fell on it. Wow, she looked terrible!

"I knew you'd be here," she said.

How? How did she know? I'd just gotten here! So much for peace.

"Going to invite me in?" she asked, lifting one foot to step inside.

I blocked her way and pulled the door closer to my body. The smell of liquor wasn't a good sign, and there was no way I was going to let her come in and make a scene.

Her initial look of offense was priceless, with her brows drawing down, her mouth forming a wide *a*. She gripped the strap of her bag tighter in her claws and settled back on her heels. "I'm surprised Lisa took you in all this time."

"She's my best friend," I reminded her. "Some people know what loyalty means."

She didn't like the dig, but too bad. She laughed. A harsh sound I didn't recognize. Like a rattle in her chest. Had it always sounded that way?

"Don't give me that loyalty crap," she slurred. "Abandoning me the way you did, with no money, bills due. I expected it from Tank, but you, my own daughter."

So Tank dumped her. If he had any sense, he'd been scared off by Marcus. "You would have let him hit me. And you lied about the earrings as an excuse to start a fight."

Her eyes flashed, and her lips zipped together in a furious, thin line.

"You brought it on yourself, Mom."

"You stole my earrings!" she shouted.

"You're wearing them."

That shut her up. For about two seconds.

"I found them again. I think Tank took them so I would blame you! He's—" She took a step back and flapped her arms like a bald hatchling. "You're upsetting me. I came here to make peace with you, to tell you I forgive you, and you're... I'm trying here."

I was far more flabbergasted than my mother pretended to be. Forgive *me*? Really?

"I know you think I'm a terrible mother."

She'd get no argument there.

"But Tank is a schemer. He took advantage of my generous nature, then tried to take over my life. It was his idea to force you to move out so he could take complete control. He threatened me. Then when you left, I let him have it. I told him you're my daughter and you come first and he wasn't going to rule me. He said there was no way you would believe I loved you, that you would turn me away when I came for you." She paused, watching my face. "Well, I see he was right about that."

She let her voice crack a little, even wiped away an invisible tear. I had nothing to say, so I let her sway back and forth, looking like a proper drunk.

"When I told him I was going to find you and bring you home, and that he could get out, he hit me, and took his things and left. Now I'm paying everything myself."

Of course. Money was always the issue.

"So, what took you so long to come looking for me?" I asked.

"I was trying to get my nerve up! I was sure you would reject me."

I nodded, still trying to process the reality that she had even come.

"And haven't you?" she asked. "You haven't seen me in ... weeks, and no hug, no invite inside. You have me standing out here like a Jehovah's Witness."

I continued nodding. What else was there to do but fall to the floor in a fit of laughter? Except this wasn't funny. It was sad and infuriating and embarrassing to think Lisa's neighbors might listen to this and know she was my mother. I was ashamed of her. I sighed, accepting the fact that I had been for as long as I could remember, and probably always would be.

She must have perceived my sigh as resignation and acceptance of her apology, because a spark lit her eyes and she smiled.

"Serena, we're family. We're all the other has. It's been that way since your father walked out."

"You were all I had," I said, grappling with a sudden eruption of anger. "I was never all you had. You had the bottle and pills."

Darkness shadowed her face for a fraction of a second before she tried to cry again. "I am sorry about that, Serena. But you know how it is. I've always been anxious, you know that. I needed something to help me relax, and it ... gets out of hand sometimes."

"Out of hand? Sometimes?" I wanted to slap her, and hopefully leave a mental imprint as well as a physical one. "Mom, you're an addict."

"I am not an addict. I have a doctor's prescription," she bit off.

"And you have one for liquor, too, I suppose." I closed my eyes briefly and held up a hand. "You know what? I'm not getting into this with you. I'm not the first person to tell you you have a problem and I won't be the last. Until you get some help, please just go away and don't talk to me."

"Your boyfriend's given you a hell of a spine, hasn't he?" she screeched, horrified that I'd dare stand up to her this way.

"It has nothing to do with him."

She looked like a light suddenly came on. "And why aren't you with him? Why are you here?"

As I contemplated telling her to mind her damn business, she walked a tight, albeit wobbly, circle in front of me.

"He dumped you, didn't he?" She let out that rattly laugh again. "Hey, I know. Why don't you see if your father's hiring? Your boyfriend might like it if you learn how to shake your ass for him." She shook her head. "He looks like a man who's been around and knows what he wants. I can't imagine why he wanted you in the first place."

"You don't know what you're talking about," I answered.

But just the fact that I answered got her attention. I don't know if it was because I was now viewing her as the enemy, or she'd always done it, but her nostrils twitched like a bear scenting prey on the wind. She aimed a laser sharp smile at me and leaned in, raising her arm overhead to brace it on the door jamb.

"The first year is hardest, then you get used to being alone," she said. "You won't like it. And speaking of being alone, I want my dog. You had no right to take Tilda."

My heart dropped to my knees at the suggestion that she would try to take my dog. Of course, I would never let that happen. "She's mine."

"Well, you keep her for now. But I'm coming to get her as soon as I can." She paused, pursing her lips and tapping her raggedy nails on the wood. "Unless you want to make a deal."

Oh boy, this should be good. "A deal?"

"You keep Tilda and I won't make a fuss...."

"If...."

"If you keep making the house payments."

This woman was unreal! How had we come to this? We'd argued—a lot—but we hadn't been strangers. Since she met Tank, she was different, nastier, and wasted more often than not. But now that I hadn't seen her in a while, she was almost unrecognizable from the woman I'd lived with all those years.

"Mom, are you on something?"

"Serena, it's only fair that you pay your share. You lived there the whole time. Don't think I won't call the police and tell them you took Til—"

"No, Mom, I mean really, are you on something? Besides Xanax and liquor?"

She shot a glance at her arm and dropped it quickly, hugging it to her side. She wore a jacket, but I would bet there were needle marks under there and I suddenly felt the wind had been sucked right out of me.

"Mom. Tell me you haven't been shooting up."

She rolled her eyes and huffed.

"Seriously, Mom. Are you on heroin now? Did Tank get you into that stuff?"

Where I thought she would get angry, she sort of just wilted, dropping her shoulders and kicking a foot against the floor. A part of me was instantly devastated. I knew what heroin did to people, how it destroyed lives so completely and that it was probably the hardest drug of all to quit. I stared blankly at a spot behind her and felt my head wagging in dismay.

"Yes, Serena, you go right ahead and judge me. You were always a goody-goody. Too uptight to have a good time or let anyone else when they're around you."

Her voice was like a rake over my nerves, digging up feelings of resentment and neglect. Not to mention the betrayal of choosing Tank over me. Her drugs over me. I shook my head firmly, refusing to let her plant any more seeds of negativity in me. God forbid they should take root and I end up as miserable as her.

"It's time for you to go," I said.

"Tank didn't get me into anything, just so you know," she said, ignoring me. "I do what I want. No one rules me."

"How can you still defend him? Still!" The sound of my voice on the rise broke the spell of disbelief, and I took a step over the threshold. "You need to look at yourself and see what I see. You're a junkie. Not like before, either. Now you look like any junkie in any alley anywhere. What next, Mom? Will you panhandle, or worse, for drug money?"

Her bony hand came back as if to slap me, but I grabbed her wrist and thrust it away. "You will not hit me. Ever."

Again, she surprised me, redirecting from anger to that faux crying thing.

"It's the drugs, Renie!" she wailed without tears, using my childhood nickname. "They make me do stupid things. And that's why I got fired and why I really need you to cover this month's payment."

"You got fired?"

"Just this one and I'll never ask for anything again."

"You've been at that store.... How did you get—"

"Are you going to give me the money or not?" she demanded, stomping a foot, all residual wretchedness erased. Incredible.

"No. I'm not giving you anything."

Part of me cringed inside. It wasn't in my nature to flat out refuse someone, least of all my mother. But another part felt okay with it, like it had when I'd changed my mind about covering for Joy ever again. Marcus might have a point.

From there, my mother began ranting, shouting something about owing her board, Tilda being tossed in the pound, and calling the police to report what Marcus had done the night I left. I didn't react to any of it, except to tell her *I* was going to call the police if she didn't leave. After I closed the door in her face, and after she gave it a sound kick with her bony foot, she stumbled away.

I guess because of the way things had gone down with us the night I left, and again moments ago, I wasn't feeling overly compassionate, or even worried about her new drug addiction. It had been a shock, but honestly, what could I do? Couldn't force her into a rehab, or go home and watch over her. I had to look at it rationally, and from this perspective, I had to let her go. I would pray for her.

I went to the couch and sat down. Sure, I would probably worry about it later, but for now, I changed my thoughts to Marcus, wishing he'd been here to stand with me. I wouldn't have this trembling, or this welling urge to scream if he was here to handle my mother for me.

But this was exactly the kind of thing he'd want me to handle myself. And I had, I guess. My hands were shaking, but I wasn't breaking into hysterics. He would be proud. Only he would never know.

I was loath to admit my mother had gotten under my skin with her remark about why Marcus would want me. As if I hadn't thought it to death already. He could have any woman he wanted. Why me?

When that question brought me back to his asking the same after our sex session, I picked up the remote and flipped channels, searching for anything to distract me from the growing ache in my chest.

CHAPTER 15

WAS TAKING A JOB guarding an American businessman in Argentina escaping from my problems? I seated my weapon in my shoulder holster. No. I don't think so. I might be here even if I'd never met Serena. It's my job. True, I had other offers closer to home, and yes, one of them paid almost as well, but that was a longer gig. This was only three weeks, one of which was up.

All right, it wasn't as though I had a reason to be home, or even on the North American continent, except to be closer to Serena, and she didn't want any part of me right now. Hopefully, I could change that when I got back, though honestly the healthiest thing I could do was forget about her. Delete all memories of the girl.

Wasn't gonna happen. Every effort to drive her further from my thoughts only imbedded her deeper. And as much as I would like to ruminate on the situation until I resolved it, there wasn't time. Carl Mitchell was waiting on the other side of the hotel door when I knocked.

"*Si?*"

"It's me, open up."

The locks clicked, and the door opened, revealing my charge, a diminutive man with silver hair and black eyes in a tan suit. I didn't know how he expected to move around undetected when his cologne was shouting "over here!" to anyone with a nose.

"What did I tell you about cologne?" I asked. "Especially *your* cologne?"

"Just a splash," Carl said. "The fragrance relaxes me."

"It identifies you."

Those interested enough to follow him through South America certainly knew his routines, his likes and dislikes. It wouldn't take a police dog to track him by his *Eau De Skunk*. Sometimes it seemed clients wanted to die, making my job harder.

"Hey, it's your life. The worst that'll happen to me if you die is ... well, nothing. I'm already paid. You.... You'll be dead. And that crap you wear makes my eyes water. I don't shoot straight when my eyes are watering."

"You have no respect for your employers, do you?" Carl asked.

"Better. I respect life, and preserving it gets harder when my employer argues with me."

He looked me up and down, slipped out of his jacket, and turned toward the bathroom. A moment later, the shower turned on. I went to the window and twitched the curtain back a little at the bottom corner. Just to see if anyone shot at me. Carl had received death threats and was definite there would be an attempt on his life during this series of meetings.

I didn't know what information he was sharing with his compatriots, whoever they were. The less I knew, the better, as far as that went. I hoped it wasn't information he'd stolen from somewhere else. I hated finding out I'd protected the wrong people. But like I said, it was my job.

Five minutes later, Carl was dried and dressed and no longer smelled like a fire in a distillery.

"Stay behind me," I ordered. "I move, you move. Don't stop for anything unless I do, don't bend or lean, just walk, and if I turn around—"

"I stay behind you," Carl announced, like a proud student.

"Right."

And what was the first thing he did when we got outside? Stooped to pick a coin up off the sidewalk.

A shot rang out.

I dove at Carl, knocking him behind a trash can as we came down on the concrete, me draped across him, gun drawn. A few women screamed and there were shouts of *"what was that?"* and *"oh my God,"* in Spanish. Carl was motionless beneath me and I scanned the area for the shooter, listening intently for the sound of approaching footsteps.

Despite the crescent configuration of the area, there wasn't a drastic echo from the shot. The origin must be back a way. If I were the shooter, I would have picked a spot on the other side of the parking lot and picked Carl off without notice, but this guy clearly wasn't professional. Thank God he wasn't, or we'd be dead. Tires squealed about fifty yards away and a maroon car sped from the courtyard. Buffoon.

I shifted off Carl and looked down. There was blood. Not so much that said he'd received a fatal wound, but still. He groaned, then started panicking, scooting against the brick building and blathering about gratitude and crazy people and other random things, one of which was "you need to get to a hospital."

It wasn't until that strange sentence hit my ear drum that I looked down and realized the blood on the pavement wasn't his. Great. Just what I needed.

I DON'T KNOW WHAT OTHER girls go through, but not one day passed in the three weeks since I lost my virginity that I didn't think about it. Not a constant stream of thought, but practically every time I passed a mirror, I checked to see if I looked any different, wondering if there were subtle ways others could tell.

I know it sounds weird, but I thought men were paying more attention to me, smiling more, holding eye contact longer. It could be I was more attuned to them now. Or it could be the new hair color—rather, my old color—all blonde. I felt different, more *mature*, and I wanted to look it.

I now had a desire to find my *sexy* self. I didn't know for sure if this was for mere exploration or secretly hoping that when I saw Marcus again, he would want me, this time for myself, not because he wanted to aid a victim.

I'm embarrassed to admit I searched the internet for some tips. I don't recommend it. Hair and make-up I could deal with. Other ideas ... not so much. Let's just say, worms aren't the only things that crawl out of that can once you pop the lid. Leave it closed. Besides, I questioned whether I even had a sexy side, or if I could develop one. Probably not, or wouldn't I have known before now?

I could talk to Lisa about it, but with her and Ted officially "together," and him being so close to Marcus, I didn't want anything to get back. To begin with, I wasn't even sure I should want Marcus back. Knowing he purposely tried to manipulate me, and wanting him anyway, was embarrassing.

Already feeling like the poster child for destructive relationships, I feared I was falling in love with him and couldn't help it. Having him hear about my efforts to become more alluring would only give him added leverage. As if he needed any.

I wondered what would happen when I inevitably saw him again. I wasn't foolish enough to believe I was so weak and would cave instantly, falling into bed, but neither was I foolish enough to forget how persuasive he was. How his hands felt cruising my bare skin, or his lips murmuring against my throat. His dark, soul-stirring eyes, boring into—

All right, that was enough. He was seducing me and he wasn't even here. I shook my hair back and fluffed a chair pillow. No more thinking about being sexy. I was going to save myself the price of hooker platforms, extensions, and push-up bras, and whatever those other things were on that one website. I shuddered at the thought. But the idea of possibly not seeing him again sent an icy shiver up my spine.

"Going to take a shower," I heard Lisa tell Ted from the other room. "You're welcome to join me."

"I would, but I don't think we'll both fit in that tub," he answered.

"Your loss," she told him, passing me with a wink on her way to the bathroom.

I giggled. Their overheard bedroom antics were definitely not helping me forget about my experience with Marcus. But I had to say they were perfect together.

When Ted came over, I tried to make myself scarce by exiting to my room and putting on my headphones. *After* dinner, of course. I couldn't force myself away from the table when he cooked. If he kept feeding me, I would gain ten pounds this month alone.

He walked out into the living room. "I'm going to run to the store. You need anything?" he asked, pulling his hat on. From the day he and Lisa met, she insisted he not wear a hat in the house, claiming she wanted all of him just the way he was, "nasty stuff and all." I hadn't known him well enough pre-Lisa to judge if he'd been a genuinely *happy* person then, but he was now.

"No, thanks," I said.

With a nod, he walked out, and I went to the kitchen to refill my coffee cup while Lisa belted out an old Backstreet Boys song in the bathroom.

I couldn't help but wonder how long our little trio could last. I was happier here than I ever remembered being—and simultaneously more miserable because of the Marcus thing—but I was already feeling like a third wheel intruding on the happy couple.

I surmised before long they would move into Ted's house, which would leave me to find another place. I couldn't afford this apartment alone, and—

Well anyway, I had to find a place I could move into with Tilda—

And, I was getting way ahead of myself.

But that's how my thoughts were coming lately. Rapid-fire, generating little bursts of anxiety that I countered continually with pauses and deep breaths. Joy kept offering me weed that she got with her medical marijuana card. She claimed she suffered from stress. Maybe if she wasn't so obnoxious, she wouldn't be stressed.

Anyway, I'd never tried it, and though the idea of using something to manage my stress was more appealing by the day, the thought of becoming my mother kept me from it.

Fifteen minutes later, there was a thump at the door. Probably Ted with his arms too full of bags to open it himself. I trotted through the apartment and swung it open.

Marcus stood in the hall, staring at me. He swallowed about the same time I did.

"H—" I cleared my throat. "Hello."

"Can I come in?" he asked. His first words to me in about a month.

I nodded, but stood still when he came forward to enter. The toes of his shoes touched my bare ones, and I jumped back. His arms shot forward as if he would grab me before I fell over or something, but pulled back before touching me.

"Oh, sorry. Come in."

I checked over my shoulder to be sure Lisa was still in the bathroom. I don't know why, other than I was incredibly nervous. He came inside, immediately filling the room with his presence, like the air itself stepped aside to make space.

"How've you been?" he asked.

For the life of me, I couldn't remember how I'd been. Or how I was right now. My head was somehow floating over my right shoulder, intent on taking in every detail of his being as he watched me with wary, dark eyes. I don't know how it was possible, but he was hotter every time I saw him.

"You look good," he said, when I hadn't spoken. "Great."

"Thanks."

"I like the hair."

I pulled on a cord of hair and gave it a stare, twirling it in my fingers before dropping it. He lowered his head and looked at the floor for a long time. I got the impression he was gearing up to say something. Knowing Marcus, it could be anything. Really. Anything. The expectation was almost more than I could stand.

"We never had that talk," he said, finally looking up.

I blinked at him. "Talk?"

"The one we should have had before you moved out."

Right. That one. The talk I thought would break my heart when he told me he'd like to keep taking me to bed, but nothing serious could come of it.

"Oh, right." I shrugged, as if it was of no consequence to me now. In truth, I wanted to hear what he had to say. Every word. Even if it would change nothing.

"Can we talk now?"

"Now?" I asked. He nodded. "I mean ... you ... you didn't give me any notice or anything."

"I know. I'm sorry about that. I've been away."

"We haven't even communicated since...." I shifted my weight to my other foot. While I wanted to hear him, this was the wrong time for a private conversation. Lisa was here and Ted would be back soon. "Now's not a good time."

"Why not?"

"Taking you up on that shower, so make room," Ted called out, coming in the door behind Marcus, not looking up until he almost walked into him. "Oh, hey man."

Marcus didn't take his eyes off mine. His face was a blank mask now, hiding his thoughts from me.

"Where've you been?" Ted asked him, carrying bags of groceries into the kitchen.

A muscle in Marcus' jaw clenched tight, and he turned and walked out, leaving the door ajar behind him.

"What's that about?" Ted asked.

I couldn't answer because I didn't know.

"Hey!" he called after Marcus. "Wait up, what's going on?"

Ted jogged out after Marcus and then there were shouts and thumps I recognized as a scuffle in the hall.

"What the f—?!" Ted shouted, disbelieving.

I ran to the hall and found Ted getting to his feet. "What happened?" I asked, wrapping my hand around his forearm, trying to help him up.

He shook my hand off and clasped his jaw. "Son of a bitch punched me. What the hell?"

Confused one second, his face changed to a furious scowl the next, before he took off outside.

I, of course, ran after him, pushing through the bottom porch door in time to see Ted fly off the stairs and land on Marcus' back. The two tumbled to the ground in a flurry of fists, dirt, and profanity.

Between punches and grunts, I heard my name mentioned, along with the words, *betrayal* and *disloyal*. Whatever had gone on, it was more than a friendly misunderstanding, and I was at the heart of it.

I'm not ordinarily so quick to fit irregular pieces together, but my brain sorted through all those random words and pictures and arranged them into a clear picture. Marcus thought Ted and I were together.

"Are you crazy?" I yelled, jumping down the three front steps and landing mere inches from the tussling pair.

"Serena, get back!" Ted ordered, just before Marcus landed a right cross on his cheek.

"Stop it right now!" I screamed.

I don't know why I did it, or how I got the height, but I launched myself at Marcus and landed on his back. Unfortunately, Ted's return fire was already headed to Marcus' face. When he dodged, I got hit. Grazed, thankfully, but enough to rattle me loose so that I fell to the ground.

"Oh my God, Serena, I'm sorry!" Ted said, falling to his knees beside me, the fight forgotten.

There were stars. Turned out people weren't always lying when they said that. Little yellow and purple ones for just an instant.

"Get away from her," Marcus grunted, kicking Ted over with a huge booted foot, then stooping to pick me up.

I shouldn't have let him, but I was dazed, and for all my exasperation with him, I wanted to feel his arms around me again. Ted didn't react to him now, only got to his feet and accompanied us to the porch where Marcus sat me down.

"Are you all right?" he asked, brushing my hair aside to inspect my cheek and temple.

"I think so." I touched my fingers to the spot I already felt swelling.

"What the hell were you thinking jumping in like that?" he asked.

"I was trying to get you to stop acting like an idiot," I told him.

"What's going on out there?" Lisa called from the top of the hall stairs.

"A couple of idiots having a fist fight!" I called back.

Lisa ran out in her pink satin robe, hair wrapped in a towel, and took in the scene. Marcus took her in, and I watched in reluctant amusement as the conclusion drew itself all over his face. He shot a glance at Ted.

"Yeah," I answered for him. "You made a fool of yourself for nothing."

"What? I don't get it, Lisa said. "You two had a fight?" She moved an index finger between Ted and Marcus. "Why?" She paused, dipped her head down and back, then lifted it and glared at Marcus. "You're Marcus, right? *Love 'em and leave 'em*, Marcus? *Take my girl's virginity and never show your face again*, Marcus?"

Marcus stood, putting Ted on alert. "It wasn't like that," he said, then pointed a finger at me. "Is that what you told her?"

I looked around, mortified. I couldn't believe Lisa had just told the neighborhood that I'd lost my virginity! Not that I knew any of the people doubtless watching from their windows, but I saw many of them every day.

"I wanted to keep seeing you. You left," he said.

"I don't want to talk about this out here," I answered.

"That's the problem. You don't want to talk about anything," Marcus fired back. "I tried to talk to you and you said you didn't want to see me anymore. Did you tell her that?" he asked, hiking a thumb toward Lisa.

"No, she did not," Lisa answered, in that scolding tone of hers, crossing her arms.

"Lisa, don't start," I said.

"You told me you were going to see where things went and then you never brought him up again, so I assumed—wrongfully, I admit," she said, crossing her hands over her heart and addressing Marcus, "that you just blew her off."

Marcus tipped his head in silent acceptance of her apology, then glared down at me. "So, you're not seeing him?" He pointed at Ted.

I shook my head, finding it a little loopy still after that swat. "Shut up."

"He's all mine," Lisa said, coming to sit by me and taking my chin in her hand, turning my face at different angles. "Let me see that. What the hell happened? Your cheek's swelling up like an egg."

"Ted punched me."

"It was an accident," Ted interjected immediately. "I meant it for him." He walked up to Marcus and punched him in the head with such force that they both reeled, but Marcus didn't swing back. "Now I feel better."

Lisa still had my face in her hand, but turned to the men. "You both better knock this crap off right now, and I mean it."

Ted slid Marcus a sidelong glance, then took a step back. Marcus shook his head to disperse the fog, I guessed. But instead of agreeing, or stating his case, turned and walked away. I couldn't believe my eyes. Really?

"Come on, let's ice this," Lisa said, and I followed her inside.

CHAPTER 16

"**W**AIT UP."

Ted jogged up beside me, but I kept walking to my car. When I tried to open the door, he held it closed.

"You don't show up to try to kick my ass and think you're just gonna leave."

"Get in."

I hit the gas before he had the door closed, half hoping to dump him out onto the curb. But it wasn't him I was mad at. Even if he'd been screwing Serena, which I now knew he wasn't. I wasn't even mad at her. I was pissed at myself.

Again.

Still.

Ted had always been intuitive when it came to me, so he knew I'd talk when I was ready. First, I needed to figure out what to say, and that was taking some time. Attacking him was one thing. Threatening to shoot him as we were rolling in the dirt was another. But accusing him of betraying me.... I had no excuse for that. It was by far the worst thing to say to a man who had devoted his entire life to the service of others, particularly his friends.

"Your reflexes are way down," Ted said, after we'd been driving about fifteen minutes. He'd waited long enough for me to speak.

"I don't expect you to forgive me," I said.

"Good."

The silence continued for another minute.

"Where are we going?" he asked.

"I have no idea."

"How will we know when we get there?"

Good question. I took the next right and headed back to where I thought the highway should be. Not that I was in any hurry to get to my empty house. I used to love solitude, but since Serena, the waiting quiet now seemed like a crouching enemy, reminding me how empty my entire life was.

"Just so you know, my reflexes are down because I spent the last two weeks recovering from a gunshot wound."

He leaned back to turn and look at me. "What? Where?"

"South America."

He looked at my crotch. "Geeze, that's rough. Sor—"

"I mean I was *in* South America."

He lifted his chin, all caught up.

"I got hit here." I pointed to my gut area. Fortunately, the bullet had nicked the lower rib, and rather than ricochet, as .22s were known to, it slowed down, causing minimal damage.

"You should've called me."

"For what?"

Ted shrugged. "It would be nice to know if my best friend was in trouble."

"Occupational hazard." I tossed him a sideways glance. "Are we still best friends?"

"Damned if I know why, but yeah."

Pride was a jagged pill to swallow, but gripping the wheel tighter helped me get it down. "I'm sorry. I shouldn't have said what I said. It was crazy."

"It was that. And it hurt, I'm not gonna lie."

I stared straight ahead.

"Never thought I'd hear those words come out of your mouth," Ted said. "'Betrayed,' 'Back-stabbing....' Not directed at me, anyway. But then, I never thought I'd see you in love either, so I can understand why."

In *love*? There it was, that big little word. The scary one that had the power to save or end a life. To turn it upside down or set it right side up.

Ted sniggered. "Anywhere around here to get a whiskey?"

"How would I know? I'm not sure where we are."

"Let's find somewhere."

"It's a little early anyway, isn't it?"

"Yeah, but I figure you need to talk—even if you don't know you do," he interjected before I could argue. "And you'll talk easier if we're both drunk."

I had to laugh. That had always been the case. Before. "I don't need a drink. But I am hungry."

I pulled into one of those chain steak houses. I figured Ted's chef's palate would revolt, but he went willingly.

"So, you and...."

"Lisa."

I nodded. "Cute girl."

"Beautiful," he corrected. "And she thinks I'm gorgeous." He grinned.

"You are," I said. "I've always found you very attractive."

Our laughter turned every head in the place. It was good to laugh again.

As soon as we'd ordered, he wasted no time prepping for his interrogation. "So, you're in love with Serena. What are you going to do about it?"

No sense denying it anymore. Not to him or myself. "Any suggestions?"

"Well, avoiding her and accusing her of sleeping with your best friend hasn't been working, so why not try ... *anything* else."

I leaned back in the chair and dropped my hands down the sides over the arms, ignoring the twinges of pain from tussling with Ted. "I want her so bad I can't sleep."

"You never were a great sleeper."

I was already shaking my head. "This is different. She's in my head constantly. And that's just thoughts of her being ... her. Wanting her in my bed is a whole other level."

Ted waved his hand in a cut-off motion. "Uh uh, we don't have to go there."

"I'm not. Only saying I want her."

"I know, *bad*, I get it."

"Did she tell you what happened?"

"About you stealing her virginity? Lisa did. Before she told the whole block. I don't know any details though, only that Serena didn't tell you she was a virgin. Man, that must've been a scene."

The scene flashed through my mind. And others. The same ones I'd been unable to prevent since that night. Memories. Sensations. I figured the only way to erase them was to replace them with different ones, which meant getting her back in my bed. Or anywhere, for that matter. I had to do things right the next time. I remembered my smug outlook on my client, Warren Peters and his lethal lover, and thinking no one gets that obsessed after a single tumble. Now here I was. But it wasn't the sex that caused this hunger. It really wasn't.

"Yeah. I handled it badly," I said. "And I more or less coerced her into bed."

"Coerced?"

"Challenged, you might say. I ended up getting what I wanted, but...."

"More than you bargained for."

That was for sure. "It started as a game. This whole damn thing from the start."

"You're not one to play games," Ted said, curious.

"I don't know, being back in the States, change of lifestyle.... Boredom, I guess. And the strangeness of it—of her—was part of the reason I started it. She's entirely too innocent and sweet for me. I was curious and wanted to play with her a little. Like a cat with a mouse."

"And we all know how the cat fares in that scenario. Didn't expect the mouse to bite back, did you?"

No, Serena didn't have fangs or claws. Yet she'd scarred me, anyway. "I was attracted to her, but—"

"You see, right there," Ted interrupted, aiming an index finger at me. "She told me you'd been in the coffee shop for months before approaching her. I found that interesting."

"What are you saying?"

"That I know how you read people. You watch them, you figure them out and then you move forward or back, accordingly. Takes you about two minutes."

"So, you think I knew I'd fall in love with her before I talked to her?"

"Stop putting words in my mouth. But...." he added, with a finger raise for emphasis, "you always said you weren't going to fall in love. Ever."

"And you think my playing with her was a subconscious attempt to have her reject me so I could have an excuse not to risk getting hurt."

"Never said that. You'd have to be smart enough to put that all together in your head first.... Oh wait. You are." He linked his hands together on the tabletop.

"That would be stupid, wouldn't it? Why would I torment myself with kissing her, desiring her, just to have her push me away?" I asked, partially because I hoped he could shed some light on it.

"I didn't say it was a smart plan," he said, then turned his palms up and shrugged. "Not that I said any of it."

No, but I'd wondered that myself during my time reflecting on it. Was it some crazy rebound thing after Heidi?

The waiter brought our food, and we ate in silence for a minute, but now that Ted had called me out on my stupidity—without actually saying it—I felt like I had to explain.

"If you must know, I told myself I was just enjoying looking at a cute girl for a few minutes while I got my coffee. Nothing wrong with that."

Ted shook his head, agreeing.

"And when I saw she was being mistreated, I had an excuse to step up. But truth is ... you're right. I think I knew from the first minute I laid eyes on her that if I got to know her...."

I stopped when Ted laughed. As amusing as this was for him, I didn't appreciate having my raw emotions ridiculed in public, like a new mother showing her baby to a stranger and having the stranger laugh and run away.

"Dude, you're making this so much harder than it has to be," he said. "Go tell her how you feel. The girl's been in love with you from day one."

"Is she? What if she just thinks she loves me? Girls get that way with sex. Over-emotional. Especially with their first. I don't want to be some kind of over-reaction she regrets later."

Ted shook his head. "She was nuts about you the first time I met her. You hadn't had sex yet."

"Sure, because I manipulated her," I said.

"Geeze, Marcus, are you gonna give yourself a break? You're acting like she's an imbecile who doesn't know her own mind. She's smart. Start over. Ask her out and go from there." Ted sawed off a hunk of steak, shoved it between his teeth, and grinned.

"What if she says no?"

Ted dropped his knife and fork on the plate with a clatter that caused heads to turn. "I can't believe what I'm hearing."

My stomach knotted. I was making myself sick. Ted was right, this wasn't me.

"I've gotten to know her pretty well and I'm telling you, manipulate her, beg her, reenact the boom box scene from *Say Anything* if you have to, but don't give her up. Now eat."

MY FACE WAS A LITTLE SORE, though the mirror revealed no egg-sized bump, just Lisa's exaggeration of a small red welt at the apex of my cheekbone. Even so, I put the ice pack back over it and let her pull my feet up across her lap on the couch.

"Marcus is hot," she said.

"Would you stop? You said that five times already."

"Well, he's hot times five."

"What about Ted?"

"Ted's hot times six," she said with a wink. "That man...." She shook her head in silent appreciation. Then she slapped my thigh. "Why didn't you tell me the truth?"

"The truth?"

"Marcus wanted to talk, and you said no?"

"Not exactly," I answered. "I was a little freaked out after ... you know. It was after I came back from here. He wanted to talk, but I told him I was moving out the next day and we sort of dropped it after that."

"Do you want him?" she asked.

"Yes." I did. I shook my head. "But he sees me as weak. I want him to accept me even if I am."

"You are not weak, Serena. You're kind and humble and generous, and anyway, he must want you, or why else would he come here? Getting a man like that to want you.... That's strength."

True, he'd come to me, and true, I wanted him more now than ever, but Lisa herself had once told me some men could get possessive after deflowering a virgin. Not only did they have to have it again, but they felt a kind of ownership.

I didn't want Marcus to *own* me, and I certainly didn't want him to treat me like a well he felt he could just dip into when the mood struck him. I wanted him to want *me*. The real *me*.

"Look." Lisa patted my leg. "You have a choice. Either accept that he won't respect you and you're just going to be his love doll until he finds someone else..."

Her *or* wasn't coming nearly fast enough for me. I lifted my eyebrows in anticipation.

"*Or* become someone he respects."

"You're telling me to change for a man? You, who's been telling me since we met that what a guy sees is what he gets and he better not expect more than you're willing to give?"

"I'm not saying change. I'm saying you can earn his respect and give him a taste of his own medicine."

"I don't know what that means."

Lisa laughed. "Not yet."

CHAPTER 17

I HOPED I WAS DOING the right thing. I smoothed the front of my clingy red dress and pulled open the door to allow Marcus entry. This plan of Lisa's, to be firm and strong, and have Marcus begging for me, would only work if he didn't do the same to me first. I had to remain impassive no matter how his impressive six-foot-one frame towered over me. No matter how good he looked in his pullover sweater and black jacket. Or his fantastic fitting pants. Or with his hair pushed back from his handsome face to frame those decadent chocolate eyes that even now were taking me in from head to toe.

I blinked and cleared my throat, which did nothing to aid my attempt to remain aloof. I had to regain the lost ground immediately, and remembering what he'd once said about his reaction to my bending over at the coffee shop, I searched for a reason to bend over. My keys were on the coffee table behind me, so maintaining eye contact with him, I half-squatted and felt around.

"I just have to grab my keys," I said, even as I made contact and *accidentally* slid them off the edge to the floor. "Oh. There they are." I straightened and turned, bending at the waist and taking my time skimming my fingers along the floor to pick them up.

I felt his gaze fastened to my bottom the entire time until I straightened up—casually, but slowly—and faced him. His lips twitched. Whether from mirth or want of something to say, I couldn't be sure. I hoped I wasn't making a fool of myself. I already felt like one.

"Are—" He cleared his throat. "Are you ready?"

Score! That one pause had me rejoicing inside. And now that I had the advantage, I planned to keep it.

"You should have a jacket. It's pretty chilly out," he said.

"I'm okay. We're going to the car, then we'll be inside." I didn't have a jacket to go with this dress, and anyway, I didn't want to cover it up and hide the view that might drive him nuts.

He followed me into the hall, pulling Lisa's door shut, then turned and took my face in his hands.

"Have to do this first."

He planted a kiss on me, quick but decisive. And just like that, he recovered his own loss and left me grasping for something to say. Fortunately, he didn't wait for me to speak before taking me by the hand and leading me outside.

On the surface, it could look like he was onto me, like his kiss had been a deliberate counter to my move, but I was probably being paranoid. I wasn't experienced in seduction—the very idea of taking the lead scared me practically witless—and he was. Really was. When he was ready to kiss, he kissed. Simple as that.

He opened the car door for me and I used all five beats it took for him to get in, to breathe slow and deep. My heart might be ready to burst out of my chest, but I refused to show it.

I didn't know if it was real or imagined, a physical thing or romantic delusion, but something in him called to something in me. Like I knew I wouldn't feel right ever again unless I was with him. I know that sounds like the basis for a warped, co-dependent relationship, but I'm not explaining it right.

He cranked the heat and pulled away before speaking, turning to me at the first light.

"You surprised me with your call."

"In a good way, I hope. I never asked a guy out before."

"I'm here," he said, by way of agreement. "That dress is pretty surprising too."

I looked down at the frilly, form fitting item. I knew it looked good on me. I made sure of it.

"But you know that, don't you?" he asked.

I would neither confirm nor deny.

"Do you want to tell me where we're headed?" he asked.

"Your place."

"*My* place."

By now, Ted would have had time to set the scene there.

The light turned, but Marcus didn't move, just kept his eyes on me until the car behind us beeped. With a slide of his palm around the wheel, he made a smooth U-turn and headed toward home.

"I don't know what you're up to, but I like it so far," he said.

"I thought we should have that talk you said I keep avoiding."

He didn't respond, and I wondered if he was the slightest bit disappointed. But he had only to wait and I would make it up to him.

"About the other day," he said. "I don't want you to think I do that. That I get jealous and do insane things like that. I'm not the jealous type."

"You're not? Seemed to come naturally." I couldn't resist the dig.

"No, I'm not. I mean, I don't mind a good fight, but that other stuff.... That's not like me. It's been a rough couple of weeks."

And it wasn't like me to be flattered by his jealousy. Or maybe it was. I didn't really know, since no one had ever been jealous for my sake before. Either way, as anti-feminist as it was—and I wouldn't say it aloud—his fighting for me made me ... hot.

"I don't like violence and bullying. But I kind of understood why you did it. It was juvenile and pointless, but I got it."

"Makes one of us."

Several times he looked like he wanted to say something, then thought better of it. I would have pulled it from him, but my brain grappled with its own dilemma. I had thought about asking him out, dressing up, and taking him to his place to have my way with him, but all this in between stuff—conversation, flirting—none of that had passed through my head. I couldn't believe I wasn't already hyperventilating.

At last, we pulled up to his house, and he turned the car off and angled in his seat to face me.

"What's this all about?" he asked. "You didn't put that on to talk."

He ran his gaze down the front of my dress again.

"Well, okay, I want to talk, but I have other plans."

"You do?" His right eyebrow arched.

"Sure, this is a date. You dressed up, too, right?" He flipped his hand over, then back. "Well, like a proper date, I thought we'd have dinner."

"Here?"

I nodded and held up a hand to stave off his next question. "It's all arranged."

"Then what?" he asked.

Okay, here it was, the moment I had to use my minimal acting skills to pretend I was sultry ... or whatever.

"Then I thought we could watch a movie. Or I'll take you upstairs and have my way with you."

His mouth opened, then slammed shut.

"I decided I want a do-over. A second chance at my first time."

His expression didn't change for a good ten seconds. Not a twitch, not a blink, until he got out of the car, came to me, and led me inside. Then we were walking through the kitchen, headed toward the front of the house and the stairs.

"Wait," I said, pulling back to look at the place settings and containers of food stacked on the counter. "There's food—"

"Ted's been here, I see."

"He helped me out," I said. "I wanted to surprise you."

"You've done that." Marcus continued tugging me through the room. "Now it's my turn to surprise you."

WE WENT STRAIGHT TO his room, where he stood me next to the bed, shrugged out of his jacket, and closed the door. There was no one else in the house, but maybe he knew it would make me more comfortable.

His gaze locked on mine as he came closer, still much taller than me, even in my four-inch heels. I tried to maintain eye contact, but time after time my eyes lowered to his chest. This was the point where I showed my mettle, as Lisa would say. It was a saying she'd gotten from her grandfather, and here I was thinking of its origin as I stood still and silent for Marcus' inspection.

Then I started thinking about thinking about it. And wondering if Marcus knew I was about to panic over thinking so much just to keep my brain occupied. I didn't know how to pretend to be a seductress! Why did I get myself into this?

"Are you okay?" Marcus asked, touching a finger to my cheek.

His touch triggered a rapid-fire nod that couldn't have been mistaken for anything other than what it was. Nerves. There was no reason for them. I knew him. I trusted him. I'd been with him before. Still....

And then he slid his hands into my hair, pulled me close and kissed me, and every worry and all my trepidation scattered like glitter in a snow globe. It was brief, and he pulled back to look down at me, my face in his hands.

"You're right, Serena, you deserve a do-over. I'm going to show you how your first time.... *Our* first time, should have been."

He glided one hand down to my breastbone, but said nothing about how fast my heart was hammering, though I could feel his hand vibrate from the force. He smiled a little before he enveloped me in his arms and kissed me again.

I had never been held like this in my life. Like I was treasured, fragile, and he was doing his best to protect me. It was surreal to have a man such as this—rugged, aggressive, huge—take such care with me. He moved his hands up and down my back, but no lower than my waist. Even when I slipped and let out a tiny moan, his hands stilled for an instant, but stayed on their chaste course.

When he'd feasted on my lips another minute, he eased his head up, but I had no power to open my eyes. My head floated like I'd been drinking wine, and heady warmth flowed through my veins, weighing my limbs down. But there was no alcohol, only his drugging kisses.

"You look beautiful, Serena."

His voice drifted to me on the periphery of my mind, finally easing through the fog and forcing my eyes open. I was losing my focus. I did my best to keep my head above water with this seduction thing, but every time he spoke to, touched, or looked at me, I felt myself sinking below the waves.

"I hope I do this right," he said. "You need to know that the importance of giving yourself like this isn't lost on me."

It was just the right thing to say, and I found my eyes welling with tears. Thankfully, Marcus didn't zero in on that as something alarming and call the whole thing off. He seemed to know intuitively how emotionally overwhelming this event was for me, and kissed me again, determined to give me the second first time I'd asked for.

Man, he could kiss. Making out with my pillow as an innocent adolescent, imagining the perfect pressure, texture, positioning, didn't come close to this. My inexperienced mind had been incapable of supplying the warmth of a man's breath, the feel of his palms heating my flesh through the thin fabric of my dress.

I'd certainly never imagined the catch of breath as his large fingers slid down my thighs to find the hem of my dress, or those slightly rough fingers lightly scraping my skin as he lifted the dress up and over my head.

The room was warm, but I shivered, standing there in my matching red panties, bra, and heels, as his gaze cruised over me, down, then up, then down and up again, lingering on particular points of interest.

"I can't believe I missed all this the first time," Marcus said, his voice a hoarse whisper. "I knew you were beautiful, but ... this...."

He smiled then and melted my heart. When he gestured me to him with his chin, I stepped into his arms, captured in their heat.

He wasn't the only one who'd missed things the first time. I stood there with my ear pressed against his chest and inhaled his scent as his heart thrummed against my cheek. It was beating faster than I would have thought for him.

After a moment, he released me and stepped back to pull his sweater off. The gasp came out unbidden when my eyes fell on the angry red scar on his stomach. He hadn't had that the last time I'd seen him shirtless. I would have remembered.

"What happened?" I asked, touching my fingers gingerly to the skin just outside the injury zone.

"Work related," he said, then took my hand and brought it to his lips. "I'm fine. Don't give it another thought."

How could I not? If I had to guess, I'd say he'd had surgery! "Work related?"

"Serena, please. Not now," he said, shaking his head.

He was right. Now wasn't the time for talk, but action. He stared at me for a few seconds, then released my hand. His sure fingers deftly unfastened the button and zipper of his pants, before he lowered, stepped out of, and kicked them aside, submitting his solid body for inspection, nearly naked but for the one remaining piece of fabric confining the hard arch of his penis.

I held back a hysterical bubble of laughter, not wanting him to get the wrong impression. It wasn't that we were both in our underwear, but the realization that the removal of these last bits of cloth would change everything. Again.

"Your turn," he said.

I felt myself coloring and didn't know why. He'd already seen everything I own. But it was time to woman-up, so I turned around to let him unhook my bra. When I did, he expelled a long breath that sent delicious shivers down my spine.

"You have the greatest ass I've ever seen."

There was no telling how many he'd seen and I doubted mine was the greatest, but I preened under the compliment and turned to face him, holding my bra in place.

"Back atcha," I said, using Ted's phrase. But when I said it, it was true.

Marcus didn't laugh, so I dropped my bra and let him look his fill, taking his gaze over me in tiny increments until I felt my blood heating. At last, when I didn't think I could stand the strain any longer, he took my hand and sat me on the side of the bed.

"Take your shoes off," he said, then reached into his bedside drawer and removed a condom.

CHAPTER 18

I DON'T KNOW WHY seeing that shimmering cellophane wrapper hit me, but it suddenly brought the reality of this soon-to-be event into sharp, dramatic focus. I was about to embark on an act that could have monumental, lifelong consequences.

And I couldn't wait.

I guess he saw my impatience in the increased rise and fall of my breasts, because he smirked and got on the bed, moving to the center, pulling me with him so that I was flat on my back, he on his side, facing me.

"I already told you I'm on the pill."

"Shh."

Gently, he brushed his lips over my cheek, his hand running over my ribs and belly, then down to remove my panties.

"You're so beautiful," he breathed against my neck. "Inside and out. I want this more than you'll ever know."

It could have been words of passion spoken in the building heat, but I believed him. To my heart, I believed him.

"Tell me you want me, Serena."

I nodded. He stroked my flesh again, and I almost purred like a cat. In fact I may have.

"Tell me."

Again, I nodded, but he caught my chin in his fingers and looked into my eyes.

"Say the words. Tell me you want me."

"I do." The words came out easier than I thought they would. "I want you Marcus."

"Only me."

"Only you."

Was it possible he knew I was in love with him? He was asking for my commitment here, and I gave it willingly. I didn't want anyone else. The thought that he might not give the same assurance if I asked him skated at the edge of my mind, keeping me silent, but all thought fled when he slid his hand between my legs and touched me.

His lips trailed scorching kisses down my throat, across my collarbone, down to my breast, where he sucked and licked, causing electrical current to run up my spine, automatically arching my back, pushing me harder into his palm. I thought I would fly straight up to the ceiling, but his mouth, now back on mine, kept me anchored until he pulled back to study me again.

"Tell me you want me," he whispered.

His breath was faster now, his tone harsher, and I wondered if he was just so afraid of hurting me or making a mistake that he wanted to be absolutely positive he should continue.

I took this opportunity to take his face in my hands and kiss him. "I want you, Marcus. It's no mistake. I know what I'm doing, and I want you to make love with me."

I couldn't express it any plainer than that, and he took my words at face value, pulling off his underwear, running his hands all over my body and devouring every moan and sigh with his hungry, eager mouth.

There was bliss. The feeling that my blood was flowing like heated honey, loaded with glitter, making my entire body feel shimmery, reflecting every spark of pleasure to every nerve ending. I swear the ends of my hair were hot.

Cellophane crinkled over the sound of his breath and he backed away to roll the condom on so quickly I honestly didn't know why I'd heard some guys made such a big deal about it.

In one fluid movement, he positioned himself above me between my bare thighs. Though his eyes were steady on mine, his breathing was uneven.

"I'm going to take it slow, okay?"

I nodded and licked my lips, determined not to make the mistake of looking down at his size and causing myself to panic. I gripped his biceps, closed my eyes, and braced for his invasion.

"Serena, open your eyes."

I did as he asked, but was still clutching him.

"You can't tense up like this. It'll hurt."

"It hurt last time."

"I know, baby, and I'm sorry. Had I known, I would have done anything to make it better for you. But this time will be different. I can't say it won't hurt at first, I don't know, but not like last time, I promise. And it'll stop right away if it does."

He kissed me sweetly, lingering until he felt my body go slack. I trusted Marcus. Of course I did, or I wouldn't be here.

"I trust you," I told him.

"I'll stop if you ask." He gave me a small smile. "But please don't ask."

He shifted slightly, pressing himself inward, so gently at first, then steadier, continuously as I felt my body welcoming him. The expectancy of receiving him fully was agonizing for me and certainly for him, until finally, he covered my lips with his and slipped his tongue inside at the same time he gave one final lunge.

He groaned into my mouth, his pleasure mixing with my cry of ... pleasure.

Yes. There was an understandable mild stretching tension, but this time it filled me with nothing but wonderful sensations, more so, as my body relaxed.

"Are you okay?" he asked, kissing me over and over, his body still for the moment.

"Yes," I breathed. And I was!

Holding himself over me, his triceps straining, he moved for several beats until I picked up the rhythm and moved with him. This coaxed a ragged growl from him and he gradually picked up the pace with no more thought for the fragile virgin, but only intent on bringing about our mutual satisfaction.

I was more than happy to collaborate as each nerve ending in my body tightened, triggering delicious ripples of anticipation, starting at my fingertips and toes, and working their way inward until they reached my core.

I shuddered, and Marcus grinned down at me. "That's it, baby. Let yourself go."

As if I had a choice when he changed position, lowering most of his weight onto me, reaching underneath to grip my butt cheeks, his speed and intensity increasing. That seething build-up in my core was nearly at the point of detonation, and I wrapped my legs around the backs of his thighs to draw him even deeper.

He complied in every way he could, sweeping me along on a vivid wave of sensation, until at last that wave crested and crashed around me and all I could do was hold on and try not to drown as my insides shattered with release.

A moment later, his lips returned to mine, his breath suspended, and he followed.

IF I EVER CAUGHT MY BREATH again, it would be a miracle. Until then, I planned to stay right where I was, pulsing inside Serena and trying to convince myself what just happened had really just happened. Well, that would have been a good plan if I wasn't wearing a condom. She pouted her disappointment when I parted from her, which, I have to admit, made me feel great.

"Be right back."

I broke a record for the quickest cleanup and returned from the bathroom to find her exactly where I'd left her, spread-eagle across my bed, out of breath, hair tussled, with a secret smile on her face. Only it was no secret how she'd gotten it.

We hadn't discussed it last time, but given my size and her lack of experience, I didn't know if I'd caused any damage, and had been worried I might this time if I didn't take it easy. But gentle and easy—though it had been on my agenda, it really had—hadn't seemed the way to go. Okay, I'd nearly lost control on that first thrust, and then when she started moving with me.... I didn't like to admit it, but that's what happened. Anyway, judging from her cat in the sun expression, she enjoyed every minute.

I got back in bed and ran a possessive hand down the length of her torso, swearing to myself that no one would have her but me. She'd said it, and I was holding her to it.

When I lifted a damp tendril of hair from her temple, she half opened those glorious blue eyes and swept them over my face before closing them again. I don't care if it sounds corny; I felt like I was looking into the face of an ethereal being, an angel, who knew everything about me from my soul outward. It was unnerving.

"How do you feel?" I asked her.

"Mmmmm."

"That's what I like to hear."

"You?"

"Same."

At once she sat up, those firm, full breasts jiggling a little as she adjusted herself. "Are you just saying that?"

I had to laugh. "No."

"Because I'll understand if it wasn't that great for you."

I opened my mouth to talk, but she plowed right over me.

"I mean, I thought you were having a good time, but I didn't know if because you were being ... careful—at least at first—maybe you weren't having that good a time, like as good a time as you would if I was ... you know. Used to it."

She actually touched my shoulder, offering me some kind of comfort. I swear I almost told her right there that I love her. Where had that come from? I pushed that thought right out of my head as fast as I could.

"I'm sorry if it wasn't ... if *I* wasn't—"

"Okay, that's all the nonsense I can take right now."

I shot my arm out, grabbed her around the waist, and slid her back to a flat position, right where I wanted her. Then I kissed her until her eyes closed again and she wrapped those slender arms around me.

"Do you feel that?" I asked, pressing into her hip. She nodded. "Good. Don't even ask me again if I was satisfied." I had to shake my head. "Come on, Serena, really?"

She answered with a light shrug and I didn't know if I'd insulted or embarrassed her, but I kissed her again. As soon as I lifted my head, she was off and running again.

"I know you have a lot of experience, that's all, and I'm not...." Her eyes went wide and earnest. "But I'm a fast learner and next time—"

I covered her mouth with my hand. "First lesson. Shut up." I started to remove my hand, but had to ask first. "Can you be quiet and let me talk?" She nodded. "And you'll believe what I say?" She nodded again, not as convincingly, but I dropped my hand, anyway. "I plan on making love to you *a lot*, so I'm not only going to tell you things that are going to make it great for you, but also for me. Does that make sense?"

"I suppose."

"So, when I say you were perfect, you need to believe me."

She nipped her bottom lip and I kissed her, hard. Apparently, she needed some reassurance.

"You were perfect," I whispered against her ear. "I couldn't imagine it better. And believe me, I've imagined us together in every possible scenario."

She pulled back to look up at me. "You have?"

"Sure." I gave her a nudge with my nose as my hand cruised over her hipbone. "Haven't you?"

She smiled. "Yes. But I'm sure my scenarios are a lot more limited than yours."

I took a few minutes to indulge myself, describing to her just what kinds of scenarios I envisioned, while dispensing more drugging kisses and lingering touches. This girl was going to be the death of me, but what a way to go.

"Give me some time, Serena, and you'll be well-versed in the art of sex," I said, rubbing the pad of my thumb over her full bottom lip. "I do have some things I'd like to teach you now, actually."

She giggled, then gasped when I dipped my hand into my nightstand drawer.

CHAPTER 19

THIS *AFTER* WAS markedly improved from the first. Marcus was attentive, gentle ... relaxed. That surprised me more than the rest. I'd never seen him relaxed before. Even when he wasn't moving or talking, he was still somehow always *ready*. For what, I had no idea, but this calmer Marcus was more approachable and when we found the energy to go downstairs to eat—him in his underwear, me in one of his T-shirts—I gave him a hug around the waist before opening a container on the counter. He gave me an odd look, but said nothing.

I inhaled the smell of one of Ted's pasta creations, now room-temperature. "This smells amazing."

"What is it?"

"I told him to surprise me. You might recognize it, it has...." I peeked inside again. "Peas, and what looks like ... crabmeat?"

"Mmm. That's his favorite. He calls it *Ted's Favorite*," Marcus said. He took two forks from a drawer and handed me one.

"Are you kidding?"

"What?"

"This is a date. We don't eat out of containers. We need plates."

He shook his head. "This is sustenance. What happened upstairs was a date."

I laughed. "This is part of it, I told you. Dinner, and then I'd have my way with you. We just did it in reverse."

He dropped his fork in the container and came up behind me, wrapping his arms around my waist and nuzzling my neck.

"I'm pretty sure *I* had my way with *you*," he said.

"That's what I let you think. I outsmarted you."

"Have it your way."

He nipped my neck, sending a shudder along my spine, and I leaned back against him with a sigh.

He chuckled. "Uh uh, you sit down, temptress, or I'm going to take you right here against the counter.

I had to admit, his thinking of me as a temptation made me feel great. But he was right, we needed food, so I sat while he got plates from the cabinet.

"So, what'll we talk about?" I asked.

He joined me at the table and shrugged, then picked up a carton and distributed pasta onto our plates.

"What do you want to talk about? This is your date. You set the tone."

I opened another carton and took out the foil wrapped garlic bread. "Why don't we talk about your bullet wound and what it is you do for a living?"

That caught him by surprise. And me a little too, finding the question still lodged in my brain after all that had happened between my first seeing it and now. Though he was still shirtless, so was kind of asking for me to ask, right?

"Why do you assume it's a bullet wound?"

"Okay, what is it? Knife? Too high to be your appendix. And the incision's too big."

"I don't want to talk about that," he said, his eyes now shuttered.

"You're not making it easy to avoid. It's right there," I said, flinging a hand toward him.

He leaned forward in the chair. Whether to block my view of his abdomen or to give more weight to his next words, I didn't know.

"Serena, don't ask me about my work. I only do what's necessary, but there are some things you might not understand."

"Like what you did when you came to my house that night?"

"And other things. Just don't ask."

I couldn't help being reminded of Michael Corleone's admonition to his wife, Kate, in the Godfather. *Never ask me about my business.* For an instant, I expected Marcus to slam his palm on the table, but he poked his fork into his meal.

We were quiet for a drawn-out moment, and I wondered if he was angry. Just when I started to ask him, he set his fork down.

"It's only because it's very stressful and the last thing I want to do is think about that. I want to concentrate on you."

On the surface, it was a fitting reply, but I knew there was so much more. Anyway, I didn't want to ruin the evening. We still had to get to know one another and I would learn all I needed to, eventually.

"Well ... why don't you consider changing careers?"

He sighed. "Serena...."

"Okay, you're right, I'm sorry. Let's talk about Sea World. Ever been?"

He laughed, which went a long way toward breaking the tension.

After dinner, we headed back upstairs to get dressed for him to take me home. I thought. But Marcus had ideas of a shower first.

"That dress is amazing," he said later, following me to the car to let me in.

"You like?" I swayed in a half circle in both directions.

"So much so I want to take it off you again."

I laughed. "I'll never get home."

"So what? Stay here." He blinked, like a man coming out of a dream. "Why am I taking you back to Lisa's anyway? Why not stay with me?"

My heart wanted to somersault, but I kept cool. Lisa warned me he might be so taken with the sex—or words to that effect—that he'd want me handy, and might even try coaxing me to move in. If I was to stick to the plan to get him to respect me, I had to refuse his offer, keep a little distance. I had to let him know my time and attention were valuable. He couldn't have me whenever he wanted.

"Uh ... I don't think that's a good idea," I said.

He opened my door, but rested his hands on top, much as he had the first time he'd driven me in his car. "Why not?"

Why not? Lisa hadn't told me what to say if he asked that, only to refuse to fall in step. But I had to supply an answer, didn't I? Well, maybe not.

"I don't think it's a good idea, that's all," I said, and angled my body past him to get inside.

"That's not an answer."

Uh oh. Maybe I could sneak text Lisa. I took my phone out, but he reached inside the car and lowered my hand. Rude, but I can't say I blamed him.

"I'm serious, Serena. We should talk about this," he said.

"It's okay, Marcus. I don't expect to have to come live with you now." I chuckled, but he didn't. It was obvious that since *he* had decided it was a good idea, *he* did expect it.

"I'm not feeling obligated because we had sex," he said.

Maybe not, but it might be my way out if I seemed to think that.

"Well, how will we really know?" I asked, making it up as I went. "You may be acting on impulse and not even realize it, and if I agreed, I couldn't be sure I wasn't doing the same. I think if we rush into something, we may regret it later."

"You aren't regretting...."

"Oh, no! No, I'm not. It's just that emotions can cloud things and we both want to keep a clear head, right?" I couldn't believe *I* had to say this to *him*. Or that I was saying it so confidently when all I wanted to do was grab him and hold on tight.

He nodded, but I knew he didn't believe me. When he got in the car, he confirmed it.

"I think you're lying," he said. My head swiveled to face him. "And that you won't stay with me because I won't tell you about my job."

That sounded a lot like I was being spiteful. Out of character for someone inclined to be steamrolled, though.

"Which tells me you don't feel you know me well enough, so you're right," he said, to my surprise.

Wait. Was he using reverse psychology to manipulate me or just trying to make me crack?

"Moving in is a big step and we might regret it." He put the car in reverse and backed down the drive. "Although we already lived together," he added thoughtfully, then paused to look at me before pulling onto the street. "I don't know what your angle is, but I'll let it be for now. And we'll talk about my job, just not today. Are you okay with that?"

"What choice do I have?" I asked, giving it a light-hearted spin. After all, I was in the habit of *'accommodating others.'*

GIVEN THE UNUSUALNESS of the situation, I didn't think I could trust either of us to know if her behavior was normal. On the surface, it seemed she was pulling back a bit. I absolutely did not want that, but if the reason for it was her overwhelmed emotions, I would just have to give her the space she needed.

It seemed like the perfect opportunity to tell her I had a job in a couple of days that might take me away as long as a week, giving her plenty of time to sort some things out. But I wondered if she might see the timing as suspect. Like I was conveniently disappearing to spite her for not staying with me.

I didn't think Serena was that way, but it was sometimes hard to tell with women. When Heidi wasn't accusing me of being *emotionally unavailable*, she had called me passive-aggressive. Passive was one thing I definitely wasn't, but I suppose it was better for her to think so than that I just didn't care about some things.

Anyway, if I had been emotionally unavailable with Heidi, that was then. I wouldn't put Serena through that. I wanted to be honest and tell her my feelings for her. But that, too, had to be planned. I couldn't risk her thinking I was acting on impulse—when she'd already expressed that fear—or worse, having her feel suffocated. I wanted to put enough time between our lovemaking and that declaration to avoid having my feelings viewed as impetuous.

"So, I'll see you tomorrow?" I asked, leaning against the apartment door. She already had the key in the lock, but I'd distracted her before she could escape inside.

She smiled and pressed her body into mine. God, I loved that.

"If you want to see me."

I tipped her chin up and kissed her for what I thought would be a minute, but two minutes later, when one kiss had turned into a make-out session, I was hot and hard all over again.

"Come back home with me," I said—well, panted—not proud that it sounded a little like begging.

She giggled against my throat. "I know you're a machine, but I need sleep."

"I'll let you sleep. After."

She planted a warm, firm kiss on my lips, turned the knob and vanished inside with a small wave. I let out a long breath and took out my cell phone. I didn't see Ted's car outside, so he wasn't here curled up with Lisa. Like I wasn't curled up with Serena.

If I couldn't sleep, neither could he.

CHAPTER 20

"HOW WAS HE?" Lisa asked, coming into my room.

I laughed. "You mean how was the date?"

She waved the question away. "Don't put words in my mouth, I know what I want to know."

"I'm not going to answer that."

In truth, I wanted to keep it to myself. Every part of it. The trepidation, the silences, the uncomfortable self-conscious moments, the passion and ... everything else. I may have been initiated, but I didn't yet feel I'd been fully indoctrinated and I wanted to enjoy this newbie stage a little longer.

"Come on, Serena, give me something," she said, climbing onto my bed. "I already know he's hot."

"Lee...."

"Just tell me if he's as good as he looks."

A squeal of laughter sprang from deep inside me and all I could do was fall back on the bed and clutch my chest while Lisa laughed.

"I knew it!" she said. "I don't know if they compare notes, but Ted is amazing and since he's best friends with Marcus, it figures, that's all. I would be happy for you except...."

Lisa liked dramatic pauses. I could do without one right now.

"Except what?"

"He's ruined you for all other men." She burst out in laughter.

"What do you mean? Because of his size?" Really? Could that happen? Already?

"No! But wait! How big is he?"

I shook my head sternly. No way was I going to describe the size of Marcus'.... Of Marcus.

Lisa straddled me, sitting on my stomach, holding my hands next to my face. "I'm not letting you up until you tell me something!"

The laughter kept me immobile more than her hands.

"I'm not kidding! We're best friends." She laughed again. "If you don't tell me something—the teensiest tidbit—I'm going to be forced to tell him one of your darkest childhood secrets."

"I don't have any."

"I'll make something up."

"Okay," I managed between breaths. "He's not teensy."

She fell off me, laughing, and we stayed that way for a minute until I sat up, wiping my eyes.

Then a thought struck me that had me cringing inside. Marcus and Ted were best friends. What if they were on the phone talking like this right now about me and Lisa? Comparing notes.

"Hey." I gave Lisa a nudge with my arm. "Do you think Ted and Marcus talk like this?"

"About women? Who knows?" she said, still chuckling, but in the next instant, sat up and stopped smiling. "He better not."

She folded her arms, putting on her thinking face, the one where she sort of stares off into middle distance and purses her lips.

"I guess it's natural—" I started.

"I don't care if it is. He better not tell Marcus what I do or how well I do it."

She left the room, and I laughed. "Well, at least it'd be complementary, though. Not about how you're awkward and sometimes a little too rough with the equipment."

Lisa ran back into the room with her cell phone. "What? You're kidding!" Then she was laughing all over again.

TED HUNG UP AND TURNED his phone over in his hands. "She warned me not to speak of our sex life for fear of being cut off." He narrowed his eyes. "Or was it of *it* being cut off?" He shrugged. "Either way."

"I don't want to know about your sex life," I said.

He chuckled. "Story of my life."

I'd never been one to brag about my sexual proclivities or adventures, but if I were, my night with Serena would become the stuff of legends. I almost made myself laugh out loud and sipped my drink to hide the curve of my lips.

"You know what that means," Ted said, tapping his phone. "They're sitting up talking about us." He wagged a thumb between us over the black enamel bar.

Hmm. I wondered what that conversation would entail.

Ted tipped his head to the side. "So, what do we do with problems?"

"Confront. Solve."

"Exactly."

"Another?" asked the barmaid, a pretty girl with straight black hair, short skirt and halter top about two sizes too small.

I shook my head, then covered Ted's glass when she tried to refill it. "He's driving."

She gave me a nod and moved on to the next customer.

"I'm not driving," Ted said. "You picked me up. I can get sloshed if I want to."

"You've had five so far. Feel anything?"

"Nah."

"At this point, why bother?"

"True," he agreed. "Just wasting money. Why'd we come here, anyway?"

I shrugged. We'd talked a little about this and that—mostly Lisa—and some about Ted's roommate, Tilda, and how he was going to be heartbroken when Serena inevitably took her. We'd had a few drinks and even touched on some past events we'd been through together. Better left buried, maybe.

I looked around the dimly lit hole in the wall. It was pretty quiet, I'd give it that much, but on a scale from *raunchy* to *classy*, this place rated *dive* at best. They allowed smoking outside, yet the smell of cigarettes drifted in every time the door opened.

Why were we here? That was a brilliant question. I guess because I didn't want to go home. My bed would seem that much emptier without Serena in it, and since meeting her, I'd decided I didn't like seclusion much anymore.

But it was still better than this place.

"Come on."

I paid the tab and followed Ted across the bare floor, my shoes sticking to spots on the scarred wood as I moved. Ted edged around a guy coming in. The guy turned as they brushed shoulders.

"Excuse me," Ted said, passing.

"Yeah, right," the guy answered sarcastically.

I knew sarcasm well. A smartass punk, thinking he'd been disrespected. Ted kept walking.

I would not kill a kid in a seedy bar in the middle of a boring as a nap town at one-thirty on a Tuesday morning. No.

Lucky for him, Ted didn't seem ruffled, and I was no longer sexually frustrated and looking to take my aggression out on someone, so the possibility the punk wouldn't have to be hospitalized looked promising.

Until he said this: "What the hell happened to your face? Mother set you on fire at birth?"

Now just why would a guy say that? And to a man half a foot taller and half a body wider, with the look of someone capable of ripping his arms off and using them to beat him to death?

Ted straightened his spine. "Excuse me?"

"You heard me," the kid said.

He was probably no older than twenty-one, and smelling of beer, now that I was close enough to breathe it in.

Ted gave him a chest bump, backing him against the wall. "I've tromped through intestines up to my calves. I earned the right to walk anywhere I fucking please, pissant."

"Don't bother with this little shit," I said. "Let his mom deal with him when she gets here to pick him up."

From there, there was yelling—the kid's—and a wild punch that didn't connect—the kid's, then some threats. Also, the kid's.

Me and Ted walked outside, and I looked around. Junior year of high school, a friend of mine taught me a valuable lesson. When you're going out drinking, never park near the bar. Bars have cameras and if something happens and you have to get away ... cameras bad. There was one on the front of the building, but I'd seen none around the corner where I'd parked.

The kid came out after us, yelling threats, his three friends in tow, but we ignored him and walked the twenty feet to the corner. The moment we turned, I pressed my back to the side of the building.

Sure enough, the kid stepped into range, and I reached out and grabbed him in a choke hold. His *friends* stopped short, turned, and ran.

"Kid, you're crazy," Ted told him, right before the boy's eyes rolled back in his head and he went limp in my arms.

I lowered him to the sidewalk, facedown, and spread his limbs, making sure his neck was straight. The pathetic lump roused even as I stared down at him.

But this was ridiculous. I wasn't in a shootout in a foreign land over corporate espionage, or shielding a client from drug dealers looking for payment, or a vengeful husband looking for blood. I was outside a bar facing off with a child. A child who may have had a gun or been exceptional with a knife. Risking my life, for what?

I decided right then I'd had enough. This was a freak situation, but putting myself in harm's way regularly to make a living wasn't worth it anymore when I now had something to live for. I wanted out.

"I'm quitting," I said, stepping over the kid and walking toward the car.

"Quitting..." Ted shrugged.

"Strongarm work."

He nodded. "Good call."

"I have a commitment to a client this week, but after that, no more jobs."

"What are you going to do?"

"Not sure yet, but I have enough to keep me going until I figure it out."

We got in the car and drove off. I still didn't want to be alone, and I knew I had a night of rolling sleepless in the bed Serena and I had shared only hours ago. I thought visiting with Tilda for a few minutes would kill some time and bring me closer in some way, but the more I turned the idea over in my head, the more I took the time to notice what I was thinking.

It wasn't at all like me to dread going home, or to want to spend time with a dog in order to feel closer to her human. I began realizing I was in more danger of Serena hurting me than of any South American guerilla or tattooed drug lord.

When we got to Ted's, I said good night and left. I had some thinking to do.

CHAPTER 21

I EXPECTED AT LEAST one message from Marcus on my phone when I woke. There wasn't. And he didn't call in the hour since I'd been up. I set the phone down again after checking it for the third time to see if the ringer was on and the volume up.

"He'll call," Lisa said, walking past me on her way to the front door.

"Sure. I know."

She turned in the open doorway. "Serena, please don't get caught up in this insecurity thing. He's into you. He'll call."

I nodded, but it must have looked as pitiful as it felt because she closed the door, walked back to me, and pulled me down to sit on the couch next to her.

"You're in the power position, remember that. You have something he wants and he'll come after it."

"I don't want him to come after *it*," I said. "I want him to come after *me*."

"Well, of course," she agreed. "But guys are really slow. They take a while to train. It could be that he's associating you with sex right now. He'll put it together soon enough that without you, he doesn't get sex."

"Or he'll go get it somewhere else."

She leaned back as though slapped. "What am I hearing? Are you thinking of using sex to lure him?"

"You're basically telling me to do that!" I said, exasperated. "But no, definitely not."

"Good! Just because you have the power doesn't mean you can wield it like that. That's handing the power right back to him."

I shook my head. Having no practical experience with relationships, I had no clue what she was talking about.

"It looks like we'll have to turn the heat up on this guy," Lisa said.

"What kind of heat?" I already didn't like the twinkle in her eye.

"Well, we already know how jealous he can be when he thinks you're seeing someone else...."

She watched me for a few seconds until her words unraveled in my head and made sense. "Oh, no."

"Yes. You need to give him a nudge."

I shook my head in definite left-right lines. "I'm not doing that. I only have to talk to him."

"Quit whining," Lisa said, with a faux slap on my shoulder. "It'll be worth it once you retrain him and he accepts you as your own woman."

"Would you do it with Ted?"

"Honey, Ted already knows who I am and how far I'll go before I pull on the reins. It's one of the things he loves most about me."

"He told you that?"

"He did."

"But I want to see Marcus! I want to be at his house right now instead of talking to you—no offense."

"None taken."

I fell back on the couch, then popped right back up. "But I won't lie to him and tell him I'm seeing someone else. He'll know that's a crock."

"Then don't lie, kind of leave it open-ended. He needs a reminder that if he wants you, chances are someone else might, too."

"You're crazy. Did you not see what happened with Ted?"

Lisa waved the comment off. "Okay, so you won't actually lie and you won't actually go out with someone, but what if you had a guy drive by? Do you know anyone who'll—"

"Risk death?" I interjected. "No. I wouldn't put some poor guy in that position."

Lisa tapped the long, polished nails of her left hand against her jaw. The other hand tapped the tabletop. "Well, we'll have to cross that bridge when we come to it. You have to be smart about it. When he calls, tell him you can't see him. That you had the plans for weeks and forgot until today. Tell him you're going to a concert or something." She snapped her fingers. "Oh, that's good! You don't have to say a word about a date. He'll know no one goes to a concert alone, and since you're not mentioning names, of course it must be a guy! Brilliant!"

"Lisa, you may be great at subterfuge, but I'm not."

She stood and patted her bag. "You get good at what you need to. Good luck."

No sooner had she left than the phone rang. Marcus. Great. So, did I practice my lying now?

"Hello."

"Hi," he said.

"Hello."

He paused. "Hi."

"Uh ... what's happening?"

"Believe it or not, I just woke up."

It sounded like it. The warm rumble of a voice not quite awake. I could picture him looking all sleepy, hair in every direction.

"Me too. I mean, not *just*, but not ... long ago," I said.

I was so nervous. And resistant. If Lisa was right—and she was most of the time—I had to refuse to see Marcus if he asked.

"Are you okay?"

"Sure. Fine. Why?" I asked.

"Something bothering you?"

"Nope. Not a thing."

He sighed. "Serena, I want to see you. Can I come over? I want to spend some time with you. And I have to tell you somethi—"

"I have work."

"Okay, then later."

"I have a date," I blurted.

The silence was long and dramatic. At least to me. I wasn't used to lying and now I was caught wondering if he knew I was lying, or was taken aback because I had a date.

"You have a date?" he asked, at length.

My palms were damp. I wiped one on the thigh of my jeans and then switched the phone to the other hand to do the same.

"You have a date."

It was a declaration that time, not a question. Like he was trying to get used to the sound of it on his ear.

"Yes," I lied.

"Now?"

"Today. Later today. After work."

"How...."

He made some sputtering sounds—like when you start a word and then stop and try it again. Several times.

"Where did you meet this guy? When?" he finally managed.

"At work. He came in and.... He asked me out."

"And you—"

Since it would be completely in line with my pretext of being a strong independent woman, but completely out of line for my character since I'd already known Marcus, I thought quickly. "It was when you were away."

"In South America?"

"Yes. Getting injured somehow doing a job you can't tell me about," I reminded him. He stayed quiet. "Well, you were gone a long time and someone asked me out. I had no reason to say no."

"No?"

"No. You hadn't been in touch, so.... Anyway, he seems really nice. Drives a BMW too, like you," I added. Oddly, I was starting to have a bit of fun with this. But his silence made me feel a little sorry for him. "Like I said, I had these plans a week ago. And it's not like it means anything."

"Cancel."

I giggled. "That would be rude. The concert is tonight."

"What concert?"

The suspicion in his voice triggered a tiny alarm bell in my head. There was no concert, but if there was, he would be there looking for me. If he'd attacked his best friend, what would he do to some poor fictitious stranger?

"You were gone a lot, Marcus. And we weren't even speaking. It's not like you reached out."

He had nothing to say to that.

After a brief pause, he cleared his throat. "It's just as well. I wanted to see you in person to tell you, but I guess I can say it over the phone.... I'm leaving on another job tomorrow. If I can't see you tonight ... I guess I'll call you when I get back."

"That would be great," I said, suddenly feeling a pit open in my stomach. How did I get out of this? I wanted to see him, but after telling him I couldn't cancel my date, changing my mind would send the wrong message. That I thought of him as more important than my own plans. But....

"I'll talk to you, Serena," he said, and hung up.

I sat there holding the phone, staring at it. What just happened? How was this supposed to help me further my autonomous self? I wanted to see him! But I'd listened to Lisa and now....

I could call him back. I could tell him I'd made up the whole thing.

And sound like a pathetic idiot. Like the kind of insecure girl he'd been trying to protect. I took in a deep breath. No. Lisa was right. It had to be this way. He had to know I wasn't at his beck and call.

But reviewing the call, I couldn't believe how cold I had sounded. At least that was the way I remembered it. He had sounded more than a little confused. And ... he was leaving! I'd been so caught up in my nerves and trying to deceive him, I had barely acknowledged that fact. The last time he left, he'd been seriously injured!

"What have I done?" I scolded myself and dialed his number.

No answer. Well, could I blame him after that conversation?

He would call me when he was back, and we would go from there.

Right?

OKAY, I SAW IT NOW. She was lying. She must still be annoyed that I wouldn't tell her about my job and had made up this *date*. That had to be it. I didn't know what to do about it except play her game. And not react. That would make her think twice about trying to manipulate me.

Though, what if there really was another guy? It was entirely likely someone had asked her out. What she said was true. I hadn't been around.

I poured water into the coffeemaker. No. There was no guy. She'd made it up and wanted me to torture myself with thoughts of another man picking her up, sitting next to her at a concert. ...watching her eyes squint a little when she smiled, feeling it in the center of his chest when she laughed. ...wrapping his arms around her ... lifting her hair from the soft skin of her neck to kiss that spot below her ear. That trigger spot that made her purr low in her throat.

"Crap."

I tore off about a dozen paper towels to sop up the water now overflowing onto the counter. She was not going to distract me with such obvious, spiteful—no, not *spiteful*. She wasn't mean in any way.... *Childish* mind games. Making boys jealous was probably one of the first things girls learned in school. It—

No. That wasn't it, either. Serena was inexperienced, but she was not childish. If I had to guess—and I did—and it wasn't about me not sharing details of my job, it could be about my asking her to stay at my place. Her behavior seemed to be about asserting herself. Not a power play, as much as drawing boundaries. Showing me she wouldn't drop everything whenever I wanted her. I understood that. But why not just talk to me?

I called Ted. He might not have the answers, but I could at least hear how my theory sounded aloud. In my head, I sounded like a self-doubting teenager. This had never happened to me before.

"She told me she has a date tonight after work," I said as soon as he answered.

"What?"

"Serena. I wanted to see her before I leave and she told me she has a date later."

"Hmm."

"Yeah. Believe that?"

"What are you going to do?" he asked.

"Nothing. I think she's lying."

"Why would she do that?"

"To make a point. Last night I asked her to stay at my place. I mean, it makes sense, right?"

"Sure it does. Handy."

I shook my head. "No. You see? I think that's what she must think. I only meant we were already living together before anyway, and she can bring Tilda there.... That's really all I meant."

"Well, yeah, that—"

"If it's not that, it could be she's mad because I wouldn't tell her about my job when she asked."

"Why?"

"I don't want her knowing what kinds of things I've done. Do. *Did*," I stressed. I'd made a genuine effort to change the way I did things. Blood wasn't always necessary. "And I'm getting out after this job. Besides, I never told Heidi what I did."

"I don't remember you mentioning her asking."

"She never asked for details. And I was with her for two years."

"That says something."

Yeah. "Did you tell Lisa?"

"That I cook? I think she's figured it out."

"About before."

"She's had no reason to ask. But if she does, I will. She can handle it. And me."

His words hit me like a slap in the head. "You think I doubt Serena can handle it?"

"I don't know. Maybe. But she might see it that way if you keep it from her."

So Serena likely doubted I respected her ability to handle difficult information. That was insulting. To both of us. "I have to talk to her."

"Guess you'll have to go to the coffee shop."

Yeah. Guess so. "Hey, she'd tell Lisa, right? If she had a date?"

"Sure, she would." Ted sniggered.

"What's funny?"

"You."

"This is not funny."

"No? I thought it was."

"Can you find out for me if she mentioned a date to Lisa?"

"How am I supposed to go about that?" Ted asked.

"You'll come up with something. See you later at the gym."

I hung up, leaving my fate in his hands. Well, I may have been a bit overdramatic.

Next, I called Melody on my pre-paid phone. We'd be spending the next week together in close quarters, with no outside contact. She's an attractive woman, and since we can't look like a woman and her bodyguard, we would pose as a newlywed couple in one room, when in actuality I would stay in an adjoining room, which I reserved.

While I went over the checklist with her, I prepped my work bag, gathering the few handguns and other items I might need.

"So should I bring lingerie?" Melody asked.

"It wouldn't hurt. In case one of the housekeeping staff gets nosy."

"When are you coming?" she asked.

"I'll be there by six a.m.."

"I'll be ready."

CHAPTER 22

"I CAN'T BELIEVE she said she has a date."

"Yeah. Weird," Ted ground out through gritted teeth.

"Why would she lie to me about another guy?"

Blowing out a breath, Ted pulled the dumbbell up again before returning it to the rack. "Maybe you're not as good in bed as you think."

"Seriously."

Ted wiped his neck with a rag and unscrewed the top from his water bottle. "Offhand, I'd say she's making a point."

"What kind of point?"

Ted guzzled from the bottle, swiping his hand across his lips afterward. "That you can't take advantage of her."

I smirked. "That something Lisa told you?" He'd already told me Lisa knew nothing about a date. Though the way he'd said she answered—*why would I know everything about her personal life?*—told me something was up.

"That, *you* told me," he said. "And I agree. Most girls want respect."

"I do respect her." I did, strange as it seemed. "But she's not the type to do this. To ... stand up for herself."

"What?"

I shook my head as a thought struck me. "She's doing more than standing up.... She's staging this whole thing. I mean, right back to yesterday. The dinner seduction, all of it. She's pulling all the strings."

"Well, you seem to have an independent woman on your hands. Lucky you." Ted laughed.

I smiled, reluctantly amused. It was manipulation at its finest.

"Yeah. Not that there's anything to *stand up* to. The most I did was ask her to stay at my house. It made sense. She was there, and we lived together already briefly."

I could say I didn't even know I was being wrangled, but that wasn't entirely true. I'd suspected early into our date that she was trying to gain the upper hand, and I'd pushed back. But I thought I had regained it. I'd assumed everything that followed had been because *I'd* intended it to go that way. Was I mistaken? Thinking about it now was mind boggling.

"Sure, it makes sense," Ted answered, curling a dumbbell with his other arm. "What makes more sense than being together?"

I paused, replaying his words, weighing them against my reasoning, and reviewing them again from a female perspective. She was translating being *together* as being *accessible*, wasn't she?

"I've never been particularly good at boundaries."

"You mean adhering to them," he corrected.

Yes, that was true. In the military, they'd been *orders, regulations*, and I'd had to follow them. In civilian life, in relation to people, they were *boundaries*, and while I laid them down, I'd never had them imposed on me.

"She wants me to be jealous and chase after her."

Ted growled, raising the weight a final time before slamming it back onto the rack.

"I'm not going to. I can't even communicate with anyone until this job is over. Even you. But I'll straighten it out."

Ted shrugged and stepped aside to allow my turn. "Maybe."

"What does that mean?"

"It means women are ... women. She may wait. Or she may say screw you."

No, not Serena. And it wasn't because she was a pushover who would hang around until I decided I wanted to see her. It was because she loved me. At least I hoped she did, even while that reality was one I still didn't know if I could handle. I knew I didn't deserve it.

Ted nudged my shoulder. "Hey, I'm kidding."

I nodded. "You know what? I'm going to cut my workout a little short."

"Good luck," Ted snickered again. "And see you when you get back."

THE DAY WAS CRAZY! I was three hours into my shift and already spent. Joy wasn't in today. Ordinarily I'd say thank God, but since I'd been firmer with her, she hadn't pestered me to do her chores or take her shifts. I smiled, thinking then of Marcus. I would tell him he was right. Eventually.

It seemed as if coffee drinkers had been shipped in by the busloads, and on top of it, I was working with a new kid—my cousin, Randy. He was a sweet guy, a couple years younger, though he looked older, and I was doing my best to show him the ropes. So far, so good, except he couldn't get the lid on a large drink to save himself. He was leaving now for his primary job, at the movie theater, and wasn't scheduled here for several days, so I'd probably have to reteach him a few things.

"Hey, how about a movie later?" he asked from the other side of the counter, bouncing his car keys in his hand.

"Sure, why not?" As usher, after taking tickets, his job was to walk around the darkened cinemas a couple times, then enjoy the movie for free. In other theaters he probably wouldn't have that kind of freedom, but his mom's boyfriend owned the place, so.... "What's playing?"

"They changed up a few, but I don't remember. I'll check when I get there and let you know."

We'd been pretty close growing up, but now that he knew I wasn't living with my mom anymore, he was obviously more into getting together. I had nothing better to do since I wasn't seeing Marcus, and now I really had a date of sorts, so didn't have to feel guilty for lying. Too guilty, anyway.

As if on cue, Marcus appeared at the front of the shop, the unexpectedness launching my heart to the base of my throat, where it stuck. Even before I'd known him—in the Biblical sense as well—and still now, I hadn't seen a more attractive man. And he was mine.

Mine. A little blade of doubt pricked me in the chest right below my floating heart. What kind of fool was I to think a man like this could *belong* to me?

After holding the door for a middle-aged woman, his gaze found mine, and he halted. I could almost swear I felt the heat of his gaze from ten feet away, popping the bubble of glee keeping my heart afloat and causing it to descend to its proper place.

Something was wrong. Well, maybe not wrong, but he looked like he had something on his mind, and it wasn't sex.

"See you tonight," Randy said, tapping the counter with a finger, then walking out.

I nodded back and looked at Marcus. "Hello," I said, adding more cheer than I felt.

I so wanted him to smile. To walk right up to me, lean across the counter and plant a kiss on me. So that everyone would see and know we were together.

He glanced back at Randy, then came to the counter, but didn't lean over. And didn't smile. A kiss seemed unlikely.

"Can we talk a minute?" he asked.

A minute? Like he was just stopping by? "Sure."

I gestured to Bill to hold down the fort, and came out to Marcus, walking him outside. Once under the gray clouds and spotty sun, I sat on the low partition wall that separated the coffee shop's driveway from the sunglass place next door.

He sat next to me and immediately bent to kiss me, pressing his lips over mine in a gesture of request and demand at once. He had a way of doing that.

When he lifted his head and looked at me, I thought he had finished, but he whispered, "My Serena," so quietly that I almost didn't hear him, and kissed me again.

This time, when he raised his head, he swiped his thumb across his bottom lip before smiling.

"You're very good at that."

"At what?"

"Kissing," he answered.

"I am?"

"And other things."

He gave me a look I felt to my core, and my heart lifted off once again. I giggled, feeling ridiculously proud, and he took my chin in his palm, cupping my cheek.

"So, I know you have a date tonight," he began.

There was no anger in his voice, and it made me wonder.

"I won't try to talk you out of it. I only wanted to tell you I'm leaving for a job in the morning and I figured I'd say goodbye now. I had hoped we could spend some time together before then, but I have a few things to do before I leave, anyway."

I found myself nodding, but oh, how I wanted to tell him the truth! Only then I would have to explain why I'd lied to begin with, and I still didn't know!

In Lisa's mind, I'm sure it made sense, as it had in mine when she'd suggested it. But now, with his warm hand on my face, his dark, fantasy inducing eyes looking into mine, then drawing closer even as they closed....

And when he kissed me again....

The guilt was overwhelming, and I gave a little shake of my head. He pulled back and sat upright.

"I guess that'll have to hold me for a while," he said.

"What?"

His right eyebrow lifted slightly. "I'll be gone almost a week. I won't have my cell, so you can't get me."

The job. Right. How quickly a kiss could knock everything out of my head! I didn't know what to say. Should I say anything? If Lisa were here, she would tell me to act cool. Just wish him well and tell him I'd see him when he got back. But she wasn't here!

"I hope it's not dangerous," I said.

He didn't respond. At all. Which concerned me a little, but also made me think I was being irrational. No comment could simply mean there was nothing to worry about. But then why not tell me there was nothing to worry about?

"I mean, you'll be careful."

He chuckled. "I'll be back. I'll miss this, though." He kissed me again, then raised his head and stared down at me. "And whatever happens ... I don't want you to be angry because I didn't tell you about my work."

"What?" What kind of thing was that to say? "What do you mean, *whatever happens*?" Was that why he was here? Because he wanted to get his *final goodbye* in just in case?

"I just got the impression you were angry about my keeping things from you."

I waved the idea away. "No. No."

"I'm getting out, anyway."

My eyes widened. "What does that mean?"

"This is my last job. Of this kind. I'm going to do something else with my life."

So, it was dangerous. Why else would he be *getting out*?

"Do you really have to go? Can't you quit now?"

He took my hand. "I have a commitment."

So great, he would go off on his mission and I would sit alone for the next week or so wondering if he was all right. Sitting alone was nothing new, but worrying about someone.... That was new.

We sat there another minute, saying nothing, until I finally stood. "Well, I guess I should get back."

I wanted him to coax me to stay just a few minutes more, but he released my hand and stood, then kissed my forehead before stepping back.

"I'll see you," he said, and walked to the corner of the building and turned.

I went back inside, but remained in a kind of daze for the next little while. He'd kissed me. Called me his Serena. But I was beginning to think he was definitely mad about my date. Why not tell me that? I didn't think he was one for games.

The urge to call him on it was almost overwhelming. I glanced over at my jacket, to the pocket, cradling my phone. If I didn't get him soon, he would be unreachable until he finished his job or whatever it was.

I even took a few steps toward my jacket, but the door rushed open, depositing a small crew of giggling teenaged girls, looking behind them and snorting. I looked for the source of their amusement. And there it was. My mother.

I tried ducking behind the counter before she could see me, but it was too late. And she'd probably been scoping me out before sashaying her way in here, looking like a marionette on invisible strings, hips swaying dramatically from side to side, arms swinging in time, jingling the sliver bracelets at the ends of her scrawny arms.

Despite her animation, she actually looked better than I'd seen her last, no longer enshrouded in that *drug-addict-on-her-last-vein* look. Well, she looked bad, but as if she'd at least put a meal or two between herself and death. Her sunglasses slid down her nose, and instead of pushing them back, plucked them from her face.

Her eyes.... Well, there was no hiding what she was there. They remained the same frightening horror movie screenshot, with shadows gouged on top of and below the sunken blue marbles, and pupils the size of dimes stuck right there in the middle. When she zeroed in on me, a sliver of ice skated down my spine.

"Renie!" she croaked, in a voice raucous enough to turn every eye to her. The question of whether she'd intended just that was answered in the next sentence. "Mommy's here. Come, give me a kiss."

She jumped half atop the counter, trying to connect her puckering lips to my face. Her lipstick was two different shades and her lips crooked and I'd avoid the kiss anyway, but it was utter shock and sheer embarrassment that had me taking a giant step backward.

My mother landed back on her feet, rocking a bit before gripping the counter's edge. "I knew I'd find you here."

She plunged a temple of her sunglasses down the front of her white eyelet blouse and shook her bracelets into an even stack at the bottom of her wrist. I had a fleeting stab of regret then.

Noreen Stalik had been so pretty once. Certainly more so before she met my father, but even as few as five years ago, she'd been able to make any man pause with just a smile. Now....

"You work so much. It's like you're always here," she said.

"It doesn't mean I have money to give you," I said, lowering my voice halfway through and sliding my eyes around the shop to see if anyone listened.

"Oh, I know that." She waved a boney hand at me and looked up at the menu behind my head. "I'm just here for coffee. I thought it would be nice to see you, that's all. It's been ... how long?"

I wasn't playing this game. "What do you want?" I asked, looking directly at her nose, avoiding her eyes. I didn't know what she was up to, but it couldn't be good.

She ordered—coherently—and I made her drink. She paused after handing me the money, but when I didn't look up, she took her change and stuffed a dollar into the tip jar.

"I'll let you get back to work."

With that, she left, and I glanced up to find the teenage girls looking back whispering behind their hands. I'd never been the object of overt mockery—to my knowledge, anyway. I didn't like it. And why should I care what a group of mean girls thought about my mother or my relationship to her? So, I wasn't protective or defensive of her. Let them judge. They didn't have to know how we got to this point.

Of course, it was probably nothing like that. I doubted the girls thought anything beyond, "look, a drug addict, and that's her daughter!" It was embarrassing to be that daughter, but more so to be the daughter who didn't feel inclined to reach out to help her mother anymore.

It might be the right thing, but suddenly knowing I didn't even share that last connection to her—that I should be the one to talk to her about getting help, or whatever—hit me like a brick. Having that connection to her had been what made me her Renie.

But I wasn't *her Renie* anymore. Now I was *Marcus' Serena*. I didn't know how I felt about that. Not about being his, but about not being who *I* chose to be. Had I switched allegiances because of *him* or because of *me*?

All at once, the air was sucked from the room and I had to get outside before I suffocated. I dared not risk seeing my mother again, so bolted out the back door in time to watch a fat gray rat dart under the dumpster. Rats didn't have mommy issues, did they? About the only testament of a good maternal relationship that I could see was that mama rat didn't eat her babies at birth. Well, Noreen had that over a rat, at least.

I leaned my head against the wood fencing and closed my eyes, remembering all the times I'd taken care of myself. Times she should have been there for me and wasn't, through neglect, forgetfulness, and sometimes, yes, even spite.

When I'd missed my whole first week of fifth grade because I had no clothes to wear—not *clean* clothes, *no* clothes—because she'd gotten into an argument with the woman who operated the laundromat and the woman refused to give up my clothes until she received an apology.

They'd been all *my* clothes, none of hers, and she'd called me stupid for not understanding it was *the principle of the thing*. Said I would understand when I got older. Well, I didn't. When my friend Lizzy—who happened to be the daughter of the laundromat owner—asked where I'd been, I'd told her. And had my clothes back that afternoon. My mother was furious.

Then there was the day I'd gotten my first period and was left to fend for myself, basing my sanitary products purchase on the recommendations of the older sales clerk at the corner store. A man.

Oh, and the day I had to beg a neighbor to let me use her car for my driving test since my mother wouldn't let me use hers because I was being selfish, knowing that my having a license would increase her insurance rates.

Beyond that were so many instances of huddling alone in the house, starving, and freezing, and bumping into things in the dark, that I really couldn't dwell on it without getting intensely nauseous.

Why did I wish there was more to our relationship than not having been cannibalized? The destruction of a great relationship would only hurt that much more.

When I felt something drip onto my sneaker, I raised my head, realizing I was crying. And for what? Wishing for a different past than the one I'd had? Pointless. All I could do was focus on my future and move forward. With Marcus.

For the rest of my shift, I replayed our exchange in my head. He seemed … off. He wasn't angry, or even unsettled about having to leave. He was just sort of … matter-of-fact. It was his personality. Like he'd explained to me once: "Assess situation. Address situation. Resolve situation."

But shouldn't our connection be more than that, even with our clothes on? There wasn't much discussion beyond his leaving for a job, and then there was kissing. Was he really just associating me with sex? Lisa would never let me live it down if he turned out to be a dirt….

No. I was letting my mind run away again. He was a decent human being….

Wow, that was lame. I'd wanted to say *respectful*. And although there was more than one way to show respect, it didn't seem to fit here. Apart from the kissing, he didn't seem that … interested.

I know it was probably the engagement with my mother making me see things that weren't there and miss things that were. One more thing to thank her for.

CHAPTER 23

S O FAR, THINGS were not going well. I'd met with Melody once in
person and had spoken with her several times by phone. She'd seemed
rational, though unsettled, considering her estranged husband was trying to kill
her. Trouble was, she had enough sex appeal to draw attention wherever she
went. Though I'd warned her twice already to blend in, she'd seen fit to wear
zebra striped yoga pants, white hooker heels, and a tight red shirt with a decal
of an arrow piercing her heart.

At first, I figured she was trying to set the *newlywed* tone, and it was
understandable. We needed to be seen and establish ourselves as a couple. But
after that initial impression, it was better people not remember us. The best
disguise was invisibility. In that outfit, she stood out. And it didn't help that as
the elevator doors closed, she leaned in close and brought my hand to her butt
so that the concierge could see.

"What was that?" I asked, stepping back.

"For looks, you know. Isn't that what we're doing here?"

I had given no thought to whether this client might actually find me
attractive. I wasn't giving it any now. "Don't go out of the room looking like
that."

"What? Why?" She looked down at herself. "I always dress like this."

"Don't. You're supposed to blend."

She twisted up her face and snorted. "Aren't we supposed to be here having
fun?"

"We're here as a couple. Anyone who knows that will assume we're having
fun. Assumptions are often stronger than visuals, anyway."

"What's that mean?"

"It means people may *think* one way and their brain goes about its business
with other things, but when they *see* something, their brain focuses on it and
before you know it, they have other thoughts."

"I—"

"Just stay inside."

She pouted. "What about going down to the restaurant? Or to the gift shop? Married couples do that."

"We won't."

She huffed and strutted off the elevator as soon as the doors slid apart. But she wasn't finished complaining and once we were in the room, dropped her butt to the bed.

"So, you plan on making this the dullest week of my life."

"If staying alive is dull, then yes."

"Well, what about room service? We can order food, right?"

I inclined my head. "But *I* order and *I* answer the door."

"So, we're pretending we're married in nineteen fifty."

She fell backward, slapping her palms on the mattress and stretching out. Whether she was trying to draw my attention to her body, I didn't know, but I turned and went into the adjoining room. The only body I wanted to see was Serena's, and that was going to be a long time coming. No job before was as long as this one would seem.

If I could, I would dial Serena right now just to have a connection with her. What was it about her that made me feel like an infatuated teenager wanting to forgo every activity, including sleep, to stay up and hear her voice? She could tell me about her favorite TV shows or facial cleansing routine and I'd be riveted.

I couldn't explain it, but when I'd walked away from her at the coffee shop.... Things weren't right. They were unsettled. I didn't like unsettled, and couldn't wait to fix whatever was wrong. Hopefully, by the end of my stint here, I'd have figured out what that was.

I must have thought about her for a half hour or more, because when I heard a knock at a door nearby, I went into Melody's room, palm cupping the grip of my gun, to find a young man delivering a food cart. He and she exchanged a few words, and laughter, and when he was turning to leave, sent Melody a wave and smile—which she returned.

"See you around," he told her.

Then he saw me. His face went blank, before his eyebrows squeezed tight together and he backed out, shutting the door.

I waited five seconds before opening the door and looking into the hall to be sure he was gone.

"What was that about?" I demanded, holstering my weapon.

"What? I'm hungry." She lifted the lid off a white plate. "I didn't have breakfast yet. You?"

"I told you *I* would order."

"Well, you went in there," she said, flinging her hand toward my room. "I didn't know how long you'd be. This sandwich is enormous though. You want half?"

"What was with that little exchange between you two?" I asked, ignoring the offer.

"That was nothing. What?" she asked, when I stared at her, waiting. "He's a guy I know. Knew." She *tsked* and flipped her hand over. "I used to date him in high school."

Unreal. What was wrong with this woman? "Did you know he worked here?"

Melody flipped her hair. "Yes. I mean, I knew he worked for a hotel, but…. Not this one," she added.

I didn't believe her. It might be nothing, but that feeling something wasn't quite right arrowed up. Maybe it had nothing to do with Serena, but with this crazy woman not caring enough for her own safety to avoid getting us both killed.

"If you let anyone else know we're here, we're going to have a problem."

She started to react to my blatant insolence—I'd been told I had that—but went back into my room and closed the door. And went out the other door.

I didn't know if I was more pissed because she'd ignored my instructions or because while a stranger was at the door—inside the room—I was daydreaming about Serena. The guy could have been her husband, or a hired killer, and he'd walked right in with me not paying attention. I'd increased the risk for both my client and myself. Yeah, it was definitely time for me to get out.

Hotel kitchen staff were ridiculously overwhelmed most of the time, so it didn't surprise me how they basically ignored strangers walking into their domain. They did so now, as a waiter in front of me slid plates from a rack, topped them with lids, and stacked a cart. The room smelled amazing and my stomach growled, confirming with some force that coffee wasn't breakfast.

The man I was looking for entered from the opposite side of the room and dropped his phone into his pocket before turning to pull a plate toward him.

"You."

At the sound of my voice, he looked over, and I gave him a follow me nod. Like a smart man, he did, into the hallway.

"Who were you talking to on the phone?"

"No one," he answered, his voice fluttering enough to tell me he was lying.

"Give me your phone."

"What?" He chuckled nervously, then straightened his spine. "Sorry, pal, don't have time for this. I'm working."

He started to move past, but I placed a hand on his chest. "Give me your phone."

He had about an inch on me, but it was more likely the miles of intent on my face that had him leaning back to retrieve his phone.

"This is crazy," he said, but handed it over. "You have no right to take a guy's phone. That's private property."

I ignored him. I recognized the number. I'd seen it stamped above several threatening texts on Melody's phone. Her husband. But I thought I'd give this guy a chance to lie.

"Who is this?"

"A friend of mine. That's all. A friend."

"Why did you call him?" Not text. Call.

"No reason. He's a friend. I don't need a reason to ca— "

The rest of his sentence crumpled in the back of his throat when I grabbed it. "I am not a patient man."

His eyes bugged out, but I released him, and he grabbed his own throat. I never understood why people did that.

"Tell me what you told him. And keep in mind it would be very unwise to lie to me."

He paused, weighing his options. They always did that, too. Finally, he licked his lips.

"They said you checked in as Mr. and Mrs.," he accused, jerking a thumb toward the lobby. "She's already married. Did she tell you that?"

There was no need for me to answer.

"She told her husband she was going away to think. Now she's here with you." He picked at a callous on his palm. "Well, I told him. I know they haven't been getting along ... and.... But he has a right to know."

If it was just her husband and not an abuser, that would be true, yes. Still, something troubled me about this whole thing and the crux of it popped into my head.

"Did she know you work here?"

He dared a step away from me and chuckled nervously. "Sure. We know each other since we're kids. She got me the job back when she was working here."

I handed him his phone and walked away, leaving him to call her husband or whatever he needed to do, as my mind fired more questions and answered them intuitively. She was playing me.

I turned it over and over in my head on the way back to the room. Melody claimed to be in the midst of a nasty divorce and that her father was dying in a hospital a few miles away. That part was true, as was the fact that she was daddy's little girl and sole heir to his custom shelving fortune.

She also claimed her abusive, soon-to-be-ex had suddenly found himself inspired to reconcile and wouldn't take no for an answer. She, naturally, wanted to be close to her father, but believed her husband would discover her whereabouts and come after her, so she needed protection. Sounded logical enough. The part she left out, however, was that he'd learn her whereabouts through her.

She told her husband she was trusting the doctors with her father's care and that she was flying to the Cayman Islands for a week to think things over, and that he'd better give her her space. According to her, he'd sworn that if she couldn't commit to coming home and giving their marriage another try, he would come after her and slit her throat on the beach.

She'd been very descriptive, and I had a hard time believing he'd use those words to force a reconciliation. But abusers were twisted and scare tactics were their bargaining chips, as long as they found another person for whom that was also currency.

Something in my gut hadn't felt right from the outset. I'd seen abused women before, and Melody didn't seem the type to scare easily.

I came in her door. She barely blinked over from the TV, pushing out the strains of a laundry detergent commercial.

"I didn't know you went out," she said.

"Went down to the kitchen."

Shoulders going taut, she clicked the remote so that the screen imploded to darkness. I stood beside her, arms crossed.

"You lied to me."

She stood, but only to move farther away before sitting again. "Okay, I did. I'm sorry. But what's the big deal?"

"I told you not to lie to me. About anything."

She shrugged. "What can I say? I didn't want you to get mad. Dave has me so sensitized at this point I'll do anything to avoid a confrontation."

She looked down at her hands in her lap, looking sad and pathetic. What was it with women attempting to manipulate me? Was I suddenly an easy mark?

When I didn't speak, she glanced up. "I knew Jayce would be here. He serves floors one through seven. But I only did it because I trust him. He's a friend, and I knew you wouldn't have to worry about a stranger coming to the door."

The more she talked, the worse her lies got. As a friend, she would know the kind of friend he was with her husband as well. Closer. She would expect him to make a call.

Which would put me right in the middle of a domestic situation that could have been easily avoided. Could have ... if she'd wanted to avoid it. Provoking it could only have one outcome.

She wanted me to kill her husband.

AFTER LOCKING UP THE shop, I headed to my car. Bill was pretty good about watching me get in safely, and he had, but he'd driven off before I remembered I'd left my phone charger behind the counter and had to go back for it.

Outside again, I thought I saw movement over by my car, but no one was in sight as I neared. Key in hand, I cleared the hood, when movement on the ground made me scream and jump back.

Someone else screamed, too.

"Hey! Hey now! You tryin' to scare me to death?"

"Mom!"

She was sitting there, forehead pressed against my driver's door.

"What are you doing here?" I asked.

"Waiting ... for you." Her breath came fast and ragged.

"Well, what are you doing down there? Are you hurt?"

I moved to help her up, and she clutched my arm, standing to her wobbly legs, using my car for balance.

"I'm wounded. Mortally. To the soul." She took in another shaky breath. "I'm exhausted. I've just run from the hotel."

"What hotel?"

"The Norfolk."

"What were you doing there?" The Norfolk was downtown, at least two miles away, and the most exclusive hotel in the area. Not a place my mother would frequent.

"If you must know, miss smarty pants, I know people over there."

Right. The vagrants who sleep between the hotel and the parking garage until they're shooed away.

"And good thing I was there. I saw your boyfriend."

"He's not my boyfriend," I said, automatically. It sounded true. *Boy*friend was a job for boys. What Marcus and I had.... That was a job for a man. I smirked a little.

"I hope he's not," my mother said. "Because I saw him with a woman. Hands grabbing, lips smacking. They were practically falling over each other to get in the elevator."

She fastened her eyes on my face, scrutinizing my reaction. My brain knew there was something wrong with the scenario she described. My heart, however, needed more detail before drawing a conclusion. So far all it said with every beat was, *she's lying, she's lying.*

He told me he was going on a job and wouldn't be back for almost a week. Was this what he was alluding to? A staycation with a woman?

"Are you sure it was him?" I asked calmly, not wanting her to think she'd gotten to me. She loved to get to me.

"Oh, I won't forget the face of the man who almost killed me," she said. She shifted her weight, leaning back on the hood, the left side of her lips curling up. "So, he's done with you, huh? I knew it."

Anger lashed inside me like a whip seeking a target. Not because of what she said, but that once again she'd said something purposely to hurt me. Why was she like this? And how could I have tolerated her spiteful scheming all these years?

"I knew from the second I saw him he was going to use you and throw you away. A man like that has a life. A real *life*, Serena. He doesn't need to be hanging around a goody-two-shoes hoping for a kiss, or whatever."

She ran a finger over her bracelets, making them clink and jingle, then tapped an index finger into the air. "He's blinded you, that's what it is. Because he's your first."

I looked at her.

"Oh yeah, a mother knows."

"That's not it," I told her.

She gave me a sneer of disbelief. She disgusted me at this point, but I didn't want to show it, so I rolled my eyes. A dead give-away, but it was the only thing I thought of.

"And this woman's not a ... *commoner*, either. Her clothes and jewelry alone—"

"Okay, we're done here." Yeah, that was it. I couldn't take any more. I wrenched my door open, got in, and slammed it. She laughed.

"I hoped now that we're both alone you'd want to get the band back together." She laughed again, a rusty sound, like a metal hinge. "I'll be back at the hotel when you're ready to look me up."

"Yeah, if I need something out of their dumpster maybe I'll run into you."

It was mean, and no matter how she tried to ignore it, I saw the slightest wince, signaling a direct hit.

What was wrong with me? How could I say something like that to my mother?! And why did some of the most life-changing conversations in my life happen in parking lots?

She recovered, though, and stood back from the car as I sped away. I wouldn't be looking her up no matter what.

My next thought was Randy. I was supposed to meet him, but with this on my mind now…. Maybe I should still go. A movie might help me dislodge unwanted thoughts of Marcus with his arms around another woman. Of his lips….

And what else would they do? Had he lied to me so he could hook up with her? Or was seducing women really part of his job? Like a spy. They did things like that all the time. No wonder he wouldn't talk about it. And why he was so good at it.

Oh my God, was he a spy? So much would make sense if that were the case. The secrecy, the long "jobs," the travelling.

The car beside me beeped, and I turned mine just in time to avoid becoming part of her passenger side fender.

"Sorry!" I yelled. She acknowledged my apology with some gesture or other, but I wouldn't take my eyes off the road again.

Yeah, I should go straight home—assuming I could get there without hitting anything. I was too distracted to sit and watch a movie. At the first light, I called Randy and left him a message.

"WHAT'S WRONG WITH YOU?" Lisa asked.

I waved a hand at her and sniffed into my pillow.

"Hey. What is it?"

She came over and gently pulled the pillow from my face. "Are you crying?"

Actually, I wasn't.

"What's wrong?" she asked again.

"I'm ... a little down." I rolled to my back and she climbed over me to lay on my left.

"What did he do now?"

"Nothing."

"Serena...."

"It's not him."

And it really wasn't. Well, of course he was involved, but absorbing my mother's betrayal had shaken me to the core. More so than I'd expected.

"My mother came to see me—well," I flipped a hand over and back. "She basically ambushed me after work."

Lisa groaned. "What is with that woman? It's the drugs, you know that." She nudged my arm. "If not for whatever she's on—"

I shook my head. My mom was definitely worse now, but it wasn't the drugs turning her heart against me. That was a character flaw she'd always had, but had controlled better.

Lisa was quiet a moment before speaking. "What did she want?"

"To tell me she saw Marcus in a hotel with a woman."

"What?"

I shook my head again.

"What hotel?"

"The Norfolk. One of the ones she lurks behind."

"Whoa, that's a nice place."

"He's working. It's a client," I said, defensively.

"You know that?"

No. I didn't. Not for sure. In my heart, I didn't believe he would ever hurt me. But ... wasn't that what most *cheated-on* parties said? That they never believed their partner would do that?

"He told me he's on a job. His last one."

"But still didn't tell you what he does."

When I didn't reply, she began rubbing my arm with long, slow strokes. It was something we'd done to help each other relieve stress since we were kids. I was grateful for it now, feeling some of the tension evaporate almost immediately.

"I'm just...." I lifted and dropped a hand to the bed and sighed. "I'm so mad at her for making me think this way."

"What way? About Marcus? What exactly did she say?"

"That they were making out in the elevator."

Lisa stopped rubbing. "They what now?"

"I'm sure it's not true, and if it is, what it means—"

"Baby, it means your man was kissing another woman."

I pushed up to my elbows. "I don't think it even happened. It's what my mother said. And I like to believe I have enough intelligence not to believe anything she says."

"I'm sure it's not true. Why would she say it though?"

"To make me suffer. It's what she's all about."

"But why now? Did she know he was going to be away? Or that he'd be there?"

"I don't even know that he is there, just what she said. It could have been someone else entirely, or it could be coincidence. She could have made the whole thing up just to be a bitch. Anyway, the thing that gets me is that she'd do that at all. What have I ever done to that wretched creature to make her treat me this way? To hurt me?"

"Nothing. You know it and I know it." Lisa gripped my forearm lightly. "I think she's jealous is what it is."

I eyed her.

"You have youth, beauty, time.... Hers is long gone. Well, she still has time, but she's wasting it. And you have a man who cares for you. Something she never had."

"You believe that?"

"Sure. I think Marcus is a little too smart for his own good at times, and thinks like most men at other times, but Ted loves the guy and that's enough for me."

She gave a decisive nod, and I giggled.

"You really like Ted, don't you?"

"*Like*?" Her right eyebrow rose to new heights. "Sweetie, that man has my heart all chained up. And he has *all* the keys. It ain't goin nowhere without him."

For a few seconds she looked like a kid again, heart in her eyes, like she had when we'd been to our first boy band concert. But she wasn't a kid now. She was a woman in love. I knew because I recognized that look in my reflection.

"But what about Marcus?" she asked. "If you weren't upset about him already, would what your mother said be bothering you so much?"

"You mean if she hadn't lied to me to tear my heart out?"

"I'm wondering if you're afraid it's true."

There might be a little room here to squabble with someone else, but not with Lisa. She knew exactly where my head was.

"Okay, let me ... it's.... It's not so much about what she said—I mean, sure, who wants to hear that. But...."

How to put this? My mother, for all of her flaws, had a way of *tuning in* to people in a way I never could. She had street smarts and could home in on people's strengths, weaknesses, defining characteristics... I was clueless and trusted everyone.

I didn't really believe he was kissing someone else—though I was damn sure going to ask him about it when I saw him—but maybe the part she said about him having a real life was true. And the kind of woman that went with his real life probably wouldn't be anything like me.

"What?" Lisa urged.

"I mean ... what if he's feeling ... entitled, because I told him I have a date? Like if I can see other people—"

"Stop that right now. The man's too grown for *tit for tat*."

Yeah, of course he was.

"Okay, then what if Marcus was spending all this time with me because he had the time between jobs? Instead of climbing the Matterhorn, he was rolling around in bed with me."

"The Matterhorn?" Lisa laughed. "Where do you get this?"

"I mean, his life is so different from mine. Like, vastly. He's been everywhere in the world a dozen times, first in the military, then as a special forces fighter or whatever you call it, and now his security job takes him away...."

"Didn't you just say this was his last job?"

"That's what he told me. But what if it isn't? Why would he stay here when he's used to wild customs, different people, foods, women? He'll get bored. Then what?"

"Your mama really got in your head." Lisa sat up.

"I've never been anywhere. I've lived in the same house most of my life. Never even had sex until him!"

I heard it. And I felt it. A slithery, edgy, creeping feeling twisting through my chest, tightening my muscles, sucking my breath away, even as it darted into my brain, accelerating my thoughts, implanting new ones. All bad.

This must be hysteria. The worst part was, even knowing its name couldn't stop it. Even knowing Lisa would only take so much before she slapped my face like we'd seen in so many movies couldn't help me from hyperventilating.

She gave me a shove, causing my eyes to focus on hers.

"Come on, kid, you're making yourself nuts."

I nodded and blinked, but she nudged me again.

"You're going to let her wreck your relationship? Cause that's what she's trying to do."

Sure, my mother would like nothing more than to see me miserable, but it was me wrecking things, not her. I was letting my brain run off, dragging these wild thoughts....

"I need a drink."

"Great idea." Lisa got up and went to the door. "How about a Manhattan?"

"I had hot tea in mind," I giggled. I wasn't a big drinker by any means, and half a glass of wine made me tipsy.

"Nah. You need something to help you relax. I have just the thing."

I followed her to the kitchen.

"Where's my grenadine?" she asked, opening the fridge.

"I thought I saw it on the door."

"Ah." She took it out, opened the freezer, and took out the vanilla ice cream.

I preferred ice cream with some texture, but when she dropped scoops into glasses, it was obvious she had special plans for it.

"Oh, wait ... do I...?" She went back into the fridge and emerged with a can of lemon/lime soda. "Yes!"

For the next minute, we talked about her cousin Janet's upcoming wedding as she performed her bartending techniques. At last, she slid a pink concoction across the table, plunked a straw in, and gave me a knowing nod.

"Where did you come up with this?" I asked.

"Drink."

"It's too nice." And it was, all pink and fizzy, with condensation already gathering at the bulbous center of the glass.

"It's a Dirty Shirley Temple."

Ah. Anything with Shirley Temple's name couldn't be bad. "There's probably not a lot of alcohol in here, right?"

"You just watched me make it," Lisa said.

"I wasn't paying attention."

"Drink." She raised her own glass and sipped from the straw.

I followed suit and was pleasantly surprised. "Mmm. This is fantastic. Tart and sweet."

"Yeah, well, I'm out of cherries and it's not usually made with ice cream, but I forgot to refill the ice trays, so we're improvising."

I went back in for another sip. "Wow, that's really good."

"I HAVE SOMETHING TO SHOW YOU."

Lisa dropped her weight on the side of the bed, dipping me to the right. My head must have kept going until it hit the floor, because it throbbed mercilessly.

"Sto-op," I whined, pressing my hand ever so lightly to my forehead. Most of the pain centered behind my eyes, and I wasn't sure I could keep them open without having them explode. "Go away."

"I will. I just want you to see this first. It may help the hangover."

"The only thing that can help this hangover is if my head falls off. My grandmother's cow, why do people drink?"

"You went a little overboard. Those DSTs go down easy."

"You kept telling me to drink!" I lowered my voice, wincing. "This is all your fault."

Lisa shrugged. "Like I said, I think this'll help."

She held her phone in front of my face and pushed the play arrow. There I was, face down on the living room floor with my hands stacked under my chin.

"*I'm not a virgin anymore,*" my slurring image announced happily.

"*I know,*" Lisa's answered.

"*You know? How do you know?*"

"*Because you told me two drinks ago,*" she answered with a chuckle, looking at me. "*And you told me the night it happened.*"

"*Then you told everybody. Every-body!*" That stupid drunk girl laughed.

My real self pushed Lisa's arm away. "Shut that off. Please. My head is killing me."

"Just a little more." She returned the phone.

"Why did you take that, anyway?"

"Because up to that point, you'd been making yourself—and me—nuts, wondering if Marcus was cheating and would forget about you."

"I was not." But it had a ring of truth.

"Yeah, you were. So I figured I'd make a record to embarrass you with on your wedding day." Lisa laughed. "Admittedly, I didn't expect this."

She turned it back on.

"*Tell me again how well-endowed Marcus is,*" Lisa's image joked.

"That's enough," I said, imagining what came next.

"*He is,*" the video said. "*He so is. He's so much sweeter and kinder than he wants anyone to know.*"

"*No, I thought you were going to tell me about his penis.*"

"*I'm telling you something better. He's endowed with amazing qualities. He's protective and loyal.... And he makes me feel like I'm the only person in his universe. Like I matter.*"

I had no choice but to tune in then and lifted my head despite the ruthless aching. In the video, I sat up and looked at the camera, and for the first time, sounded sober.

"I never knew love could be like this. All those romance novels, and...."

Drunk Serena went to the couch and stretched out. Closed her eyes.

"The paper heroes in those pages are nothing like him. For the first time in my life.... I feel loved."

A few seconds later, a shadow fell over my image and Lisa turned her camera to Marcus standing there looking down at me! I took a quick breath, watching as he kneeled beside me. Kissed my cheek. And whispered—not thinking anyone could hear— *"I do love you."*

When he turned to Lisa, she stopped filming.

"What happened?" I asked now, reaching for the phone.

"That's it." She shrugged. "I didn't want him to see I was filming him. But then he picked you up and carried you in here to put you to bed."

I looked around the room; I guess to check he wasn't still there. Silly, but I was pretty sure I was still tipsy. My head seriously felt like it would explode, but it was slightly better when I closed my eyes.

"I don't know what your plan was, but it didn't help me feel better."

"Do you need to throw up again?" Lisa asked.

I slitted one eye open. "Again?"

She nodded, the movement of her head making me dizzy. "You barfed for about ten minutes."

"Oh, Lisa, I'm so sorry. Did I mess anything up?"

"Don't worry about it. Marcus cleaned everything up. Including you."

I pushed to a seated position, regretting it instantly. "What?! He was here for...?"

"Yeah. Sorry. No footage of that, though."

An image of Marcus handing me a towel flickered in my brain. At first, I thought I was recalling a dream. But when the images began flashing regularly....

"Oh no. So ... he really watched while I hung my head in the toilet?"

"'Fraid so."

Lisa brightened and stood, jarring me once again, making me feel like my ship was about to capsize.

"But, hey, now at least you know he's good in a crisis."

"I already knew that," I said.

And now he probably thought I had the propensity to be a drunk like my mother. I didn't—never planned to drink like that again—but it would be the obvious conclusion. Like mother, like daughter.

"Why was he even here? He's supposed to be working."

"He left," Ted said, coming into my room.

Oh great. Another voice. I must look an absolute wreck, but I felt too lousy to try to fix myself up. I only hoped— "Marcus isn't here, is he?"

"No."

I took a relieved breath. My head throbbed.

"You're in a bad way," Ted said.

"Good call, Captain Obvious," Lisa chided.

His laughter didn't help my head any.

"I have just the thing." He turned to Lisa. "You have baking soda, right?"

They walked out of the room together, leaving me in my misery, mostly because of thoughts of Marcus seeing me in that state. And cleaning up after....

As the minutes passed, memories I would have supposed drowned bobbed to the surface.

Marcus coming into my room and pulling the sheet up to my neck.

Murmured words.

Him calling me *baby*—in the good way.

Me telling him I lov—Oh no!

No. No. No. I dropped my heavy head into my palms. Had I really told him I love him? Stinking drunk and smelling of puke?! He'd said it to me, but that was before I'd.... Why would he say that, anyway? Humoring the drunk?

Beneath the steady static of pain came the more intrusive whir of the blender in the kitchen, scattering my already jumbled thoughts. A moment later, Ted came and handed me a glass filled halfway with thick brownish gray liquid.

"Drink this."

"That phrase got me into this situation," I said.

He lifted his chin, and I did as I was told. Surprisingly, it didn't make me want to throw it up again. It was sweet and a little gritty, but tolerable.

"I won't ask what's in it."

"Good."

Ted took the glass and turned to go.

"Ted."

He looked at me.

"Why was Marcus here last night?"

"I'll let him tell you that," he answered, whistling as he left.

CHAPTER 25

IT WAS HARD not to regret sparing Serena's mother's life. Even harder not tracking her down now and demanding she tell her daughter the truth about what she saw—*didn't* see—on that elevator. Apparently, she'd told Serena I was hooking up with Melody, and according to Lisa, Serena had been wondering how much of it was true. Yeah, if I saw that scrawny....

I was glad Ted told me what was happening. While finding Serena passed out was surprising, it was good to hold her again. Holding her hair back while she spewed into the toilet wasn't fun, but she probably wouldn't remember it today. She told me she rarely drank, so I could only assume news of me and Melody had brought it on.

Ted suggested I let her suffer in silence with her hangover and give her a chance to refresh herself before going over, so in the meantime I reviewed some files and follow-ups, and decided to return Melody's fee. Technically, I didn't owe her, since it was her fault the job had been terminated, but I hadn't put myself out that much. Besides, if her husband ended up maiming her, she'd suffer enough. If he killed her.... Oh well. I wasn't responsible for anything that went on in that relationship.

I had a dozen calls to return, and it was time for a haircut, but after an hour of sitting on my back deck staring at the mountains, I conceded I wouldn't get anything done today and headed to Serena's.

Lisa opened the door with that knowing glint in her eyes and led me to Serena's room. She wasn't laying down when I walked in, but was showered and dressed, and there was no remainder of the mess she'd been last night.

"What are you doing here?" she asked from behind her new desk by the window. Well, old desk. Ted had had it at his place for years.

"I'm here to see you, obviously."

"I mean, why aren't you on your job?"

I didn't care for the way she said *job*, drawing out the latter portion to give the word more weight than necessary.

"May I?" I asked, closing her door whether or not she wanted me to.

She rose from the chair, and I wasted no time cajoling her to come to me. I went to her, took her in my arms and swept a hand across her left cheek and into the hair behind her ear. Then I kissed her, long and deep, feeding myself as well as her, and telling her without words how much she meant to me.

When I lifted my head, her eyes remained closed for another moment as her tongue lightly skimmed her lower lip, ending with a light scrape of her teeth in the left corner.

I kissed her again, and was instantly treated to a mental image of her naked, writhing beneath me. I knew what she looked like under these clothes, how silky her long, slender thighs were, how soft the short hairs at the apex of those thighs. I knew her butt cheeks were the perfect size for my palms, that they were springy and smooth and firm. That her stomach was an even plane of soft skin that rippled into taut muscle when she tensed with the pleasure of orgasm.

Damn, I was already hard, my breath clogging in my lungs from trying to keep a normal tempo. Hard to do with the fire now raging in my blood, and the emotion that just seeing her had abruptly dosed into my bloodstream. And along with it, the memory of her telling me she loved me. I needed to hear those words in the bright light of day.

The catch in her throat warned me I was doing something wrong—or right—and I loosened my hold. Now wasn't the time for lust. Of course, glancing down at her bright eyes fixed on mine, that was easy to forget. I slid my hand down to hers and pulled her to sit beside me on the bed.

"How are you feeling?"

She colored instantly. "Much better now that I've showered. And Ted gave me something...." Then she shook her head. "Marcus, I don't want you to think.... I don't drink like that."

I smirked, but she squeezed my hand, serious.

"I mean, I don't want you to get the impression I drink when I'm stressed. Lisa made these Shirley Temple things—"

"*Dirty* Shirley Temples," Lisa corrected through the door from the hallway.

Serena and I glanced over.

"What are you doing?" Serena called out.

"Eavesdropping," Lisa answered. "Would be a lot easier if the door was open."

Serena snorted. "Fine."

Lisa opened the door and came in, followed by Ted.

Serena rolled her eyes and looked at me. "Anyway, the drinks were really good."

"They were," Ted corroborated.

Serena shot him a dirty look. "But I didn't expect them to be so strong." She flung a hand out toward Lisa. "She kept making them for me."

Lisa smiled. "She needed to relax. And what's a friend supposed to do?"

"Anyway, they got the better of me and I guess that's when you came in. I don't remember a lot."

"Not even throwing up," Lisa said.

"Yeah.... Sorry for that, by the way," Serena told me. She lowered her head. "I just didn't want you to.... I didn't want you thinking—"

"That she's an alcoholic like her mama," Lisa finished for her.

"I don't," I said. "And I'm sorry if I upset you somehow."

"That really wasn't it," Serena said, then amended her statement. "I was upset ... thinking about some things I probably shouldn't have been, but I didn't get drunk to forget my troubles or whatever."

"They just go down easy," Lisa said.

"They do," Serena agreed with a nervous giggle.

I glance at Ted with an imperceptible nod, and he draped an arm over Lisa's shoulder.

"Come on. Let's leave these two alone."

Lisa paused, looking at Serena.

"The rest of what I have to say is private," I said, gesturing to the door with my chin.

When they closed the door behind them, and Serena blinked up at me, I started leaning forward for a kiss. But it would have to wait. I straightened and gripped one of her hands in both of mine.

"Why were you upset?" I asked.

She took her time and sighed, preparing to tell me everything. I hoped.

"Because my mother.... I just don't get why she does the things she does to me."

Hmm. Not what I expected her to say. But I knew why her mother did those things. Because she was so far entrenched in her wretched lifestyle, she couldn't crawl up, only try to pull others down. The tremor in Serena's voice warned me she might cry, so I didn't say it. Fortunately, she sniffed, stiffened her spine, and went on.

"I've basically taken care of myself, and her, since I was eight. Why can't she be thankful, and, if not be nice, at least stop making things hard for me?"

Her large blue eyes were full of heartbreak and genuine curiosity.

"I would have been in nursing school already if not for having to pay for practically everything in that house. And when I think about it, I teeter between depressed and really pissed off."

I wanted to tell her that was fine, but it wasn't.

"You're right," she said, surging to her feet. "You've been right about everything. I let everyone push me around, decide for me, coerce me.... I could be so much further ahead if I wasn't a dopey idiot."

"You are not an idiot. You're a sweet person." There couldn't have been a cheesier thing to say, but it fit her like no one I'd ever met. "You're kind and considerate. Maybe overly so. It stands to reason you'd let people go too far. But now that you know and can properly direct it.... You're a force, Serena."

Her bottom lip trembled, but she still didn't cry. "The thing of it is...."

She paused, and I got the impression she wasn't sure if she should continue.

"Is...." I urged, moving my hand in a come ahead gesture.

"It wasn't just my mother. I mean...." She flattened her palms on an invisible surface in front of her. "Look, you may dump me eventually, anyway, and that's fine, but—"

"Whoa, what?" Dump her? Was she crazy? I opened my mouth to ask, but she talked over me.

"I'm not that pushover anymore, and I think I have a right to know about your job and what goes on."

"You do."

"And I know it's really stupid to come out and say these things right out loud, giving you an advantage—again—but I don't want you to hide things from me, and I don't want to hold back and make you wonder, or play senseless games."

My eyebrows rose.

"I didn't have a date, Marcus. There's no ... other guy. Nobody. Nobody but you."

"Then who was the kid at the shop? He was leaving when I came in." Good thing I'd restrained myself from grabbing him as he passed.

She huffed and rolled her eyes, and I fell in love with her all over again.

"That was my cousin, Randy." She shook her head, not wanting to be interrupted. "He works there now. And just so you know, I really wasn't trying to make you jealous, like to mess with your head. I just wanted you to know I don't need you to ... complete me."

"And that you won't tolerate me expecting sex from you whenever I want it. Message received."

She looked at me, stunned. "Uh ... yeah. Did you talk to Lisa?"

The question confirmed she'd probably gotten the foolish idea from her.

"I figured that part out all on my own." I took her hand and stroked her fingers between mine. "I get it. I do. And I'm sorry. I know you're concerned about my safety. Rightfully so." I placed a palm over the healed wound on my abdomen. "You were right about this. Bullet hole."

She winced, and I made myself smile.

"I'm good as new, so you don't have to worry," I added quickly. "So, I'll tell you now everything out on the table. I protect people for money. Sometimes it's dangerous. I usually didn't have to hurt anyone, but if I did ... I did. I tried not to kill them, depending on what part of the world I was in."

I paused for a sigh. "And the only reason I didn't tell you was because I didn't want you to think I don't have a conscience. I don't want you to see me as that guy you thought I was when we met." I looked her in the eyes. "I can live with everything I've done, Serena. I just wasn't sure you could."

She looked like she was processing this information and I let her. Several seconds later, she took her hands back and picked at her nails.

"And this job is something you ... enjoy?"

Did I enjoy it? Hmm. Now that I thought about it, no, I never had.

"I did it because I had the skill and the time. Sometimes I hated it more because I couldn't stand the humidity, or the client was a lying criminal, or an unfaithful sleaze. Or lately, because I wanted to be here. With you."

Her expression.... Disbelief. Confusion.

"And let's get this out there once and for all," I said. "No. I've never had sex with a client, or anyone involved with a job. And, if it helps, I was completely faithful to Heidi when we were together. I don't sleep around like that." I hooked a knuckle under her chin and nudged her to look at me. "Nothing happened with the woman I was just with. Not even kissing. In fact, I figured out pretty quickly she was using me to murder her husband, and I left her there. Quit on the spot."

"You left her there?"

I couldn't tell from her tone whether she was happy or surprised I'd walked off that job.

"I admit I made a mistake. Leaving you and taking the job was stupid. I don't need the money."

She nodded, but lowered her head, looking at her feet. "So, what will you do now? I know you're used to traveling all over. Now what?"

"I'm going to sit on my back deck and relax. Finally."

She gave me a half smile.

"And when I'm not on the back deck, I plan to be in bed with you."

She looked like she wanted to say something else, but didn't dare. It took me a minute to realize exactly what that was.

"Why did you bring up my dumping you?"

She took a half step away, but I pulled her forward to stand between my knees.

"I'm...." She took in a breath and feathered it out between her soft lips. "I'm being silly, I guess."

I knew she was only saying that to placate me. "Serena, tell me what's on your mind. Honestly."

She sucked in another quick breath and let it out. "I'm wondering if you'll get bored and start to feel trapped!" she blurted.

Bored? Trapped? "What?" A blast of anger tightened my chest and clamped my teeth so that I had to force my mouth open. "Did your mother tell you that, too?"

Her eyes told me all I needed to know. I couldn't believe the balls on that woman. I'd almost shot her and her slimy boyfriend to death and she wasn't afraid to run her lying mouth? But anger had no place right now. Not when Serena might think it directed at her.

"It makes sense," she said. "We have nothing in common. You've been everywhere. I've been nowhere. We don't even have that in common, nothing to talk about."

"Are these doubts your own or ones your mother put in your head?"

I'm not sure what happened then. She'd been all ... girly and on the verge of weepy one second, and the next, looked up at me clear-eyed and somber.

"Yes, she brought it up, but it was something I've thought about before. I don't understand how someone like you could want me. I mean, why? Really."

I stood in front of her. "That might be the stupidest thing you could have said."

She gave a delicate shrug with one shoulder, then lifted and dropped her other arm and I swear if I wasn't afraid the air mattress would pop....

I paused. Now it was my turn to be tentative. Coming clean was one thing, but.... Okay.

"I'm going to tell you something I didn't even want to admit to myself," I said. "I was a little intimidated by you in the beginning."

Her brows tugged together. "What?"

"I came into the coffee shop and saw you, and yeah, you were hot and everything, but something about you struck me from the first minute. I watched you talking to people and serving them, and doing your job and I thought no way was I going to get involved with you. I thought you were too good for me." Her look of absolute astonishment had me chuckling. "Turned out I was right."

"I'm ... but...." She shook her head. "You're...."

This rabbit hole of insecurities was one I wouldn't go down now, for both our sakes. And since it was about impossible to make a flustered woman understand the reason, I had to gain her complete attention first. I took her face in my hands. That small, bright, perplexed face.

"I am in love with you, Serena. I'm willing to set aside my self-doubt and fear of inadequacy and hold on tight to you because you're too amazing to let go."

That actually coaxed a laugh from her. True, it was a tad maniacal, but I'd take what I could get.

"Now, I've said I love you, but you haven't yet. Sober, I mean."

For as much as I felt in control, I was equally at her mercy. If she really didn't feel the same, there was nothing I could do about it. She'd told me last night, but in the same breath, also confessed an unnatural fondness for gummy bears, and an urgent desire to join Seal Team Six.

I thought a kiss might pry it from her, and brought my lips toward hers, but like an eel through a net, she slipped away.

"Okay!" She held her hands up, holding me off. "Okay. I'm going to tell you the truth now and.... Do with it what you will."

One of my eyebrows arched, and I inclined my head calmly, though inside I thought my heart might just stop dead.

"I never had anything to lose," she said. "Well, except for Tilda, I never had anything in my life worth trying to hold on to. And then you showed up and made me want something I didn't even know was a ... a thing! I mean, who are you?! You're gorgeous, sexy—" she shook her head. "You came in, and for whatever reasons, you're interested in me. Me." She placed a hand on her heart. "And now, for the first time in ... ever, I'm scared to death of losing something. I have to tell you, Marcus, I am not a fan of this feeling."

"Just say it, Serena."

She closed her eyes and shook her head. "I don't think you're getting—"

"Say it. Tell me what you want."

She lifted one delicate hand and let it fall, hopelessly. My heart was trembling, fearing what she would say next.

"What I want more than anything.... Is for you to stop treating me like I'm broken."

A bucket of ice water would have done no better to stop me cold. Broken?

"Broken?" I asked. "I do that?"

She nodded. "You're always trying to fix me. And no matter what else I feel, that's always there, underneath. This fear that if you don't simply tire of me, that I'm going to do something to push you away."

I came to stand in front of her. "Baby, I don't think you're broken."

"Then why have you been so intent on changing me?"

She lowered her head, and the impact of her words slammed into me full force. That's what I'd been doing, yes. I'd changed her from a timid doormat to a strong, vital woman. But it didn't mean she'd been broken to begin with, only that my monster ego thought she should be the way I wanted her. If I was glad of one thing, it was that she wasn't anything like I'd envisioned. She was so much more.

I let out a long, exasperated sigh and tipped her chin up to bring her eyes back to mine. "Serena, I'm sorry. Looking at it now ... it seems that way. But I think you're the most perfect creature on earth. You always were."

"You mean except for my terrible habit of being nice to the undeserving," she said with a self-depreciating giggle.

I shook my head. "No. Without your generous heart, we wouldn't be here. You gave me chance after chance I don't deserve. I don't think you're broken in any way." I shrugged. "Well, except in your ability to pick men. I'm an ass." She gave me a slight nod of consent. "I only wanted to see you stand up for yourself. But now I see that's my issue, not yours. You're sweet and compassionate, and sometimes it kills me to watch you bend so far to accommodate people who don't appreciate you. That's something I have to deal with."

I couldn't tell from her lack of reaction what she was thinking. It could range from *I don't think this is going to work out,* to *you are the most egotistical, manipulating piece of crap I have ever met.*

When she took my wrist and removed my fingers from her chin, I braced for whatever might be coming. I wasn't expecting this.

"I didn't know this side of you existed," she began, with a slight tremor in her voice. "This ... exposed soul."

"Yeah, I'm a little surprised myself. I've never been in this place before. All I can do is ask you to forgive me for making you doubt my feelings, and ask for a chance to...."

Sheesh, I sounded like a Hallmark movie. Was I this pathetic?

Yes. In this moment, yes. Of all the scenarios I'd envisioned, I'd never seen myself vulnerable, or Serena in control.

"Give me a chance to love you the way you deserve to be loved. I need you, Serena, exactly the way you are. You are my weakness."

In the next moment, I had my arms full of warm, giggling woman.

"I love you, Marcus," she said, her head against my thundering heart. "So much it steals my breath."

She backed up and smiled. That flirty, beaming smile that brought its own light. So, she'd wanted me to state my commitment first. And I had. More of those boundaries. It was fine by me. I was desperate for her and would do whatever I had to to prove myself to her.

"You really are something, my Serena," I said without vehemence, only a legitimately earned sense of awe and respect for her. "You've got me here admitting you're my weakness and that everything I have is yours."

"I don't want everything you have," she said. "I want everything you are."

In that moment, I knew how she must feel, and it knocked me off balance for a few seconds. She wanted *me*. All of *me*. I didn't even want that. I hung my head, humbled.

"I am all yours."

She laughed, then kissed my chin, my lips, my cheek. "So, it looks like you're stuck with me. Be gentle."

Then she whispered in my ear.

"But not too gentle."

~ THE END ~

THANKS SO MUCH FOR reading! If you have a moment, please consider leaving a review. They're so important to authors!

Looking for Fantasy, Romance, and Adventure with Kings, Captives, Faeries, even a Sasquatch or two? Check out HEART of the KING! (Formerly published in sections as Kings & Captives, Faeries & Warriors, and Princes & Traitors)

CONNECT:
https://www.facebook.com/DanaPratolaAuthor
https://www.instagram.com/danapratolaauthor/
www.DanaPratolaRomance.com[1]
(Don't forget to sign up for my Newsletter!)

---

1.   http://www.DanaPratolaRomance.com

Also by Dana Pratola

DESCENDED
Jett
Sebastian
Aaro
Ulrick

Standalone
K-I-S-S-I-N-G
Like a Country Song
The Haunting of Josiah Kash
Weakness
The Covering
I Kissed Kevin's Girlfriend
Heart of the King